This Book Belongs

To

· ·

THE CHRISTMAS ANGEL

*

THE
CHRISTMAS
ANGEL

Jane Maas

Line Drawings by Abbie Zabar

THOMAS DUNNE BOOKS
St. Martin's Press
New York

THOMAS DUNNE BOOKS.
An imprint of St. Martin's Press.

Illustrations copyright © 2013 by Abbie Zabar

www.stmartins.com

Design by Kathryn Parise

LIBRARY OF CONGRESS CATALOGING-IN-PUBLICATION DATA

Maas, Jane.
    The Christmas angel / Jane Maas. — First edition.
        pages cm
    ISBN 978-1-250-03757-2 (hardcover)
    ISBN 978-1-250-03758-9 (e-book)
    1. Christmas tree ornaments—Fiction. 2. Domestic fiction.
3. Christmas stories. I. Title.
    PS3613.A17C75 2013
    813'.6—dc23

                                                    2013024085

St. Martin's Press books may be purchased for educational, business, or
promotional use. For information on bulk purchases, please
contact Macmillan Corporate and Premium Sales Department
at 1-800-221-7945, extension 5442, or write
specialmarkets@macmillan.com.

First Edition: November 2013

10 9 8 7 6 5 4 3 2

For my two sisters Susan

THE
CHRISTMAS
ANGEL

*

PROLOGUE

✳

My great-grandfather Owen Thomas, a young coal miner from Llanelli, Wales, visited London in December 1875. According to family legend, while he was watching a play, he fell head over heels in love with the beautiful young actress playing a small role. He went backstage and proposed to her on the spot.

This is his story, and the story of the angel he carved for the Christmas tree he believed they would share. How the angel crossed the sea and was handed down in my family from one generation to another.

I have written it as truthfully as I could, based on letters and journals and family lore. Some of the dialogue and actions are imagined, based on my knowledge of the characters and what they might say or do.

This is a story of faith and love. Yes, and magic, too.

And of the miracle that brought the angel home again.

PART I

Christmas in Wales, 1875

He had scrubbed himself hard, but he worried that there might still be traces of coal dust under his fingernails. Owen scowled as he inspected them. Homesick for the coal mine, is it? he asked himself. Well, you'll be home again in Wales and back in the deep dark before you know it.

He peered down at the stage from his seat in the balcony. The place seemed magical to him, the city seemed magical; he had never even dreamed of coming to London. And when, just a month ago, the men's choir of St. David's learned they had won a trip to London to sing in an eisteddfod, he thought it miraculous. They had come in third in the contest, in a field of forty-three groups from all over the kingdom. They didn't call it an eisteddfod here in London, though; they called it a singing contest. Eisteddfod is better, he thought. The word sounds more like music.

All London was talking about the beautiful young actress making her London debut in this play. Jessica Lavery. The girl with the lavender eyes. Not the starring role, but the kind of riveting cameo that makes an impression. Owen had heard about her, read about her in the press. He accepted, as part of the magic, the theater ticket to the matinee urged on him by the wealthy sponsor who underwrote their travel to London.

The curtain rose. Jessica Lavery made her entrance. Made her speech. Made her exit. Owen did not breathe. When the curtain fell, he and the other men from his choir stood and clapped furiously. As Jessica stepped forward to take her solo curtain call, Owen took a deep breath and shouted: "Brava! Brava!" He had read that "brava" was the proper term of praise for a female singer. He hoped it worked for an actress as well. He called it out again, and Jessica Lavery smiled up at the balcony.

Owen pulled on his coat. "Shall we have some tea?" his

best friend, Dai, was asking the group. "Not for me," Owen told them all. "I am not for tea. Today I am for adventure. I am on a quest."

The doorman barred the stage entrance. "Your card?"

"I don't have a card," Owen stammered, introducing himself. "I just want a few minutes with Miss Lavery."

"You and the rest of London." He looked Owen up and down. "Ah, why not, come on in. It's almost Christmas. Just write down your name and address for the record." Owen complied, and the doorman led the way to a door marked simply No. 3. He knocked, opened it, and announced: "A Mr. Owen Thomas from Llanelli, Wales." He pronounced it with an "L" sound, as in "love."

"Flanelli," Owen corrected automatically, and entered the small room.

Jessica turned to the door, transfixing him with a look. Her eyes really *were* lavender.

"Yes?" she asked.

Every word of English left him, and he spoke in the first language he had ever heard.

"Oh, you must be speaking Welsh, and I'm afraid I don't understand it. Could you translate, please, for a poor, uneducated Englishwoman?"

"I said, 'There is beautiful you are.' " He found his voice, remembered why he had come backstage, and grinned at her. "So we will be having Welsh lessons around our fireside."

"Whose fireside is that?"

"*Our* fireside. You are the most beautiful woman in the world, and I have fallen in love with you. It is like an enchantment woven by Merlin, that you and I will spend the rest of our lives together."

Jessica had experienced ardent stage door admirers before. Usually, with the help of the doorman, she would quickly usher them out. This time, in spite of herself, she wanted to hear more. There was something about this dashing young Welshman that intrigued her. "But Mr. Thomas . . ."

He ignored the interruption. "As an actress, you surely cannot ruin the plot of an Arthurian romance," he teased.

Her tone began to match his. "Surely you are precipitate, sir."

"Surely there is precedent, madam. Dante fell in love with Beatrice the first moment he saw her, and loved her for the rest of his life. When Romeo first sees Juliet he asks himself, 'Did my heart love, till now?' "

Jessica's eyes widened. Perhaps he is an actor, she thought. Actors are vulnerable to impulses like this. He looks untamed, somehow. Maybe he is a poet. That's it. He looks like the portrait of the young Byron in the National Portrait Gallery.

"Thank you, Mr. Thomas, you pay me a great compliment. But it's the theater you have fallen in love with, not really with me. You are in love with the role I'm playing, the sweet young innocent. And you will surely meet and marry someone just like her."

"Not someone *like* her. Someone who *is* her."

"But I am an actress. I have already made my vows to belong to the holy order of the theater." She decided to try a different subject, something that might bring him back to reality. "What do you do in Wales, Mr. Thomas? Dare I guess that you are a teacher?"

"After I finished at the National School, I thought of continuing my studies and becoming a teacher. For the moment, until I decide, I am in the coal mine in Llanelli."

"Have you only those two choices then? You seem to me a man who could do much."

"Ah, sometimes I think so too. Hubris, Miss Lavery, hubris, a trait I do not detect in you. Yes, I do have a third choice, another humble one. Ever since I was a little lad, I wanted to own a farm; to be part of nature, to make things grow. There is nothing fresh and green about a mine. Do you know Wordsworth?"

"Only a little."

"We will read him together by that fireside of ours. But first

I will take you to Llanelli and show you the magic of Wales. To Saint David's to see the enchanted well of Saint Non, which sprang from the earth the day she gave birth to David. The place in the Preseli Hills where Merlin quarried the bluestones and flew them through the air to form Stonehenge. The only places in all of Britain where those stones are found are the Welsh hills and the circles of Stonehenge. The geologists say that the Ice Age moved them. But we Welsh know better."

"I am sure you do." Jessica smiled.

"And we will visit the tomb in the hills where King Arthur lies, although he is not dead but only sleeping until the day when Britain needs him and he will rise from his sleep to lead us once again."

"Is Wales always full of magic?" Jessica was falling under his spell.

"Always. And in exactly one week it will be Christmas, the most magical time of all. The streets are full of music, the mines ring with it. The carolers are out every night, even when it's bitter, and people fling open their doors to listen and invite us in to have a drop and warm ourselves at the fire."

"Does your family have a Christmas tree?" Jessica asked. Queen Victoria and Prince Albert had imported the tradition from Albert's Germany, and decorated trees were the rage.

"A Christmas tree in front of the fireplace?"

Owen shook his head. "My father believes that a Christmas tree must always be *outside*, where it can look up to God. But here in London you have your own Christmas traditions. Tell me, Miss Lavery, do you have a tree? Do you have carolers?"

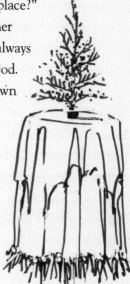

"A small tree, on a small table. And the carolers have begun to sing in the street where I live, in Kensington Square, near Hyde Park. But they have not yet sung my favorite carol, 'O Come, O Come, Emmanuel.' "

"I do not know it. Why is it your favorite?"

"Because it calls for us to rejoice. And that is what Christmas is all about."

The stage doorman knocked, and two men entered, crowding the little room with cigar smoke and laughter. They laid hats and walking sticks on a side table and tugged at the snowy cuffs of their shirts peeping from their expensive tweed jackets. Owen put his hands in his pockets, ashamed of the coal dust he imagined might still cling.

Introductions were made. The Londoners gave Owen a glance, assumed him harmless. "You were even more splendid than usual today, my dear," one said.

The second visitor chimed in. "We must do supper after the theater again tonight. We will be waiting with a carriage as soon as the curtain comes down. The oysters at Claridge's are splendid." His gaze flicked to Owen. "But you are from Wales, Thomas. You be the arbiter. Which are better: the oysters of Swansea Bay or the oysters of Brittany?"

Jessica, irritated by the dismissive tone, intervened. "Mr. Thomas is from Llanelli." She was careful to pronounce it correctly. "It is famous for its music, but not for its oysters." Owen listened in wonder as she continued, "But now you must excuse us. Mr. Thomas has invited me to tea before the next performance, and to a place I enjoy so much that I could not refuse."

When they were alone again, he felt bolder. "Oysters, is it? I will spread oysters before you, with pearls in them, every one. But where am I taking you to tea?"

Jessica laughed and opened a picnic hamper. "This is the tea we will share, if you are willing. It is simply cold jellied chicken with bread and butter, something light to eat between the matinee and the evening show." She poured tea and set out the food.

Owen lifted his teacup in a toast to her. "Welsh tradition has it that every good Welshman pays his debts before the new year begins. So I must try to repay your hospitality very quickly."

The lavender eyes shone at him. "I do believe, Mr. Thomas, that somehow you will find a way."

The next afternoon, a Sunday, Jessica was in her sunny bedroom at her writing desk, grateful for an entire day without performances. "I woke up this morning thinking of Wordsworth," she wrote a school friend who lived in the Lake District. "And of course my thoughts turned to you." It was a quiet time in Kensington Square, as were all Sundays, so she was surprised to hear a bustling in the street. There, just beneath her window, was Owen, standing in front of a group of some dozen men. He was the tallest, she thought, and the most handsome. She threw open the window and heard Owen announce: " 'O Come, O Come, Emmanuel.' " The men began to sing, in nearly perfect four-part harmony. As the carol ended, with its great final burst of "Rejoice!

Rejoice!" Jessica opened the front door. She stood there, not minding the cold, while they sang "Good King Wenceslas" as an encore.

"Will you all come in and warm yourselves?" she asked Owen.

"We are not coming in, but you are coming out. I am taking you to tea at Claridge's."

"But I cannot— "

"Please do not delay. I have used the prize money from the singing contest to rent a hansom cab. But I can afford only three hours." Owen grinned at her.

He has won again, she thought, as she grinned back. "I will fetch my cloak."

They drove along Kensington Road, skirting Hyde Park, where a few gentlemen were out riding in Rotten Row. "How did you all happen to know my favorite carol?" Jessica asked. "I believe you told me yesterday that you were not familiar with it."

"Last night, just before I fell asleep, it came to me that we could serenade you with that carol. So this morning I turned my friends out of bed early for rehearsal. And there we were."

"Do you always act so swiftly on impulse, Mr. Thomas? Is it a Welsh trait?"

"I believe it is a Thomas trait. We do everything quickly. Like rising to occasions. Falling in love."

"It is a trait known as speed at grasping nettles."

"My dear Miss Lavery, you can hardly be classified as a nettle."

The streets were thronged with people, all preparing for the coming holiday. Costermongers were out with their barrows, one selling fruit, another vegetables, yet another sweetmeats. They saw a man selling roast chestnuts, a woman selling hot eels; a knife grinder, a muffin man. And everywhere there were buskers, playing fiddles or banjos or simply singing. Their hansom trotted up Park Lane, past Grosvenor Square, into Brook Street, and drew up before Claridge's.

The doorman, resplendent in a great fur hat, approached the carriage. "But perhaps you are tired of Claridge's?" Owen suggested. "You were here just last evening with your friends."

"They are not *friends*," Jessica corrected him quickly. "No, I did not join them. It seems that our little picnic gave me all the nourishment I needed." And, she added to herself, perhaps more than I expected.

The doorman handed her down from the carriage, and Owen escorted her through the lobby, decorated with festoons of pine and garlands of ivy. When they entered the lounge where tea was served, there was a hum of surprise;

some of the patrons recognized Jessica and speculated about the young man at her side.

As they drank their tea, Jessica noticed how Owen cradled the fragile cup. His are strong hands, she concluded, but gentle, too. Tender enough to hold a child. Or a woman. Stop imagining things, Jessica Lavery, she scolded herself, and bit into a scone. "You have more than repaid my hospitality for cold chicken, Mr. Thomas."

"Ah, more is to come. There is another Welsh tradition that is centuries old. When a young man declares  his intentions to a young woman, he carves her a spoon. It is called a lovespoon. And by accepting it, she says, with no words needed, that she accepts him."

"A spoon?" Jessica smiled.

"But you deserve something more dramatic, more theatrical. When we are at home in Llanelli I will carve a great 'J' for Jessica. And put it over the door."

"Just like royalty. Like a Tudor."

"Oh, Tudors were plain Welshmen. No, for you we need a grander dynasty. Nothing but Plantagenets for you, it is."

They talked intently for an hour. He told her more of Wales at Christmas. Of how they believed that at midnight on Christmas Eve, the animals could talk together, and anyone who was born on a Christmas Day could understand them. Of how, on that day, his entire village rejoiced and was glad, just as the hymn directed.

"I should like to be in Wales for Christmas one day," she murmured, half to herself.

"I will come back to London in one year's time, and gather you up and take you home."

"An entire year, Mr. Thomas?" Jessica tried the teasing tone again, hoping they might be able to laugh together about his infatuation. "What will you be doing all that time?"

"Falling even more in love with you. And building a cottage for us. A white cottage in a glen. With a Christmas tree outside the door." Again, he grinned at her. "And a nursery inside."

The lavender eyes shone at him. "Mr. Thomas, there is something about you that is quite irresistible."

Llanelli
Christmas Day, 1875

My dear Miss Lavery,

You told me I might write to you. I hope that you will write to me.

I sang in our chapel choir at the Christmas Eve service last night. And sang again this morning. The entrance hymn is one of my favorites, set to an old Welsh tune known as "Bunessan."

> Child in the manger, infant of Mary,
> Outcast and stranger, Lord of all,
> Child who inherits
> All our trespasses,
> All our demerits on Him fall.

The Irish and the Scots claim this tune, as well, but it is Welsh to the core.

The whole Thomas family was at the table to eat the Christmas dinner my good mother prepared. Mutton—there is nothing better than Welsh mutton—three vegetables (winter vegetables from our root cellar: carrots, sprouts, and celery) and potatoes boiled with leeks. Two puddings to finish—a plum pudding and a lemon syllabub.

There are five of us, my three big brothers—Davey, Huw, and Thomas—and my little sister, Branwen. Not a one of us married, so all of us boys put our weekly pay in our mother's apron every Saturday. And every Saturday she gives us our spending money and a lecture about how not to spend it. You might think it is strange for grown men to act so. I am twenty, and my brothers are all older, but that is the way of it in Wales.

The women mind the money and the men mind the women.
Even my father hands over his pay.

After dinner, Davey and I walked the path along the
Wern—that means a marsh. It was muddy underfoot from all
the rain, but the sun was shining, so the townfolk were out to
enjoy the weather. Everywhere along the way, people smiled
and bowed and wished each other Nadolig Llawen. That means
"Happy Christmas."

When you come home with me to Wales, cariad, I shall
teach you Welsh. So in the evenings we can read aloud together
from the old tales of Arthur and Owain and the Knights of the
Round Table. Great warriors they were, and many a damsel
they saved from dragons, or evil sorcerers, and protected their
honor with great vows sworn on their swords. As I would
protect yours.

I am, Miss Lavery, yours in all things,

Owen Thomas

London
1 January 1876

Dear Mr. Thomas,

We have two performances today, a matinee and an evening
performance. So I am writing this letter to you after the one
and before the other, in my little dressing room, where we shared

the cold chicken. As soon as I finish this letter, I will have cold chicken again, although it will not be as tasty, this time, without the Welsh spice.

Mr. Thomas, I must beg you again not to be so serious in your prospects for any relationship between us. You honor me, indeed, but please understand that my life is completely dedicated to being the best actress that I can be. And, if possible, the best actress of our time, although I know that is hubris. (Yes, Mr. Thomas, I know the word, so there is one thing, at least, that you do not have to teach me.)

However, if I ever need a champion to protect my honor, you would certainly be my choice as knight errant.

Please write to me again. If you wish to do so.

Yours most sincerely,
Jessica Lavery

Llanelli
10 January 1876

Dear Miss Lavery,

Serious about our relationship? I have never been more serious about anything in my life. Last Sunday, after chapel, my brother Davey and I set off to find the place where we will build our house, the house you and I will live in together. And find it we did.

*The land belongs to my uncle, my father's brother, Lloyd
the Smith, as he is known here. He will give me the plot and five
years to pay for it. It's a fairy glen, with a brook that sings your
name, and a fir tree just outside where the house will stand. At
Christmas, we can decorate it, and it will look straight up to
God.*

*My father and brothers and I will build it. My good mother
and my sister will sew the curtains. My mother has warned
me to ask you, however, if you would not prefer to sew them
yourself.*

Yours most truly,
Owen Thomas

London
20 January 1876

Dear Owen Thomas,
*I beg you to stop this madness. I implore you to come to your
senses. I told you when we first met that you were too hasty in
your assumptions. I have never said that I will marry you.*
I am not able to leave London and the theater.
I do not even know how to sew.

> Llanelli
> 1 February 1876

Dear, dear Miss Lavery,

    You have never said you will not marry me. And I will teach you how to sew.

    We will begin to build as soon as the ground thaws. I am going to call it Glan Wynne—the White Glen.

> Devotedly,
> Owen Thomas

> Llanelli
> 13 February 1876

Dear Miss Lavery,

    There has been no letter from you in these two weeks. My heart is darker than the mine.

> With the deepest concern,
> Owen

> Llanelli
> 20 February 1876

Jessica, my little one,

    Are you ill, cariad? Shall I come to you?

> Your very worried and loving Owen

London
25 February 1876

Dear Owen,

Please forgive my silence. I am so sorry that I caused you any worry. The reason is: our play has a new leading man. We have been busy rehearsing these past weeks, preparing for him to take over the part. Mr. Brent, who played the role when you were in London, has left for New York. He was offered the starring role in a drama written especially for him, and the offer of fame and fortune was too great for him to withstand. So, sadly, he has deserted the West End for the lures of Broadway. I will never do that. I will never leave the theater, and for me London is the theater.

I sit here at my writing desk, look out at the square, and remember you and your friends singing to me to rejoice. Yet today, for some reason, I feel sad.

Believe me, yours most sincerely,
Jessica (Lavery)

P.S. I have tried to find the meaning of cariad, *without success. I assume it is Welsh.*

J.

Llanelli
1 March 1876

Dear Jessica,

In chapel yesterday, we sang a fine hymn, "Now Praise We All Our God." And I praised Him, indeed, that you are not ill.

Today is Saint David's Day, and every loyal Welshman wears a leek in his buttonhole or on his hat. (The leek is the symbol of Saint David, who lived in the Black Mountains, drinking only water from the stream and eating nothing but wild leeks.)

I am writing this letter to you at five of the morning. It is still dark, but I have an hour's walk to the mine, so must be on my way.

This winter has been long, but the little flowers of the spring —crocus and daffodil and my favorite, the snowdrop—are pushing up through the earth, so soon we will begin to build.

Your devoted,
Owen

P.S. Cariad *is indeed Welsh. It means* "beloved."

London
9 March 1876

Dear Owen,

I read your letter again this morning in the sunlight from my window, and thought of you walking to your mine in the darkness. Is it already dark when you return home? Please tell me what a day is like for you in Llanelli.

It seems I cannot prevent you from building the house in the glen. I hope it will be beautiful and blessed, and that one day you will be proud to bring your bride there.

Your true friend,
Jessica

Llanelli
18 March 1876

Dear Jessica,

I will be proud indeed to take my bride to our home, but you are the only woman who will be mistress of that house.

You ask me what my day is like. When a man works in the mines, there is not much day in a day. As you know, it is dark when I walk to my work, it is dark in the mine, and dark as we go home.

I will tell you of the mine in a few words. It is a tormented place, a hell of ice and blackness, a scene from Dante. Cold, it is, because we are below the earth. Wet, it is, because the underground streams run through it. We men work the seam, great pieces of coal fall to our axes, and the mule drivers pick them up, put them in the carts, and take them to the shaft. (The mules live all their lives down in the mine, and never see the sunlight, but strong and healthy they are, and happy, and better cared for than most of us men.) At the entrance of the shaft, the breaker boys—the young lads, younger than fifteen, not yet strong enough to wield an axe—break the big pieces into smaller ones. Then the coal is winched to the surface.

At half after six in the morning, the whistle blows and we go to work. At noon the whistle blows, and we eat the cold lunch in our pails. At half after twelve the whistle blows again and back we go. At half after four the whistle blows a last time, and we ride the car to the surface.

Those are the good sounds of the whistle. Sometimes there are the bad sounds—the sharp blasts, one after another—that all in Llanelli can hear, and all dread to hear them. It means there is trouble below: fire or flood or cave-in. I pray I will not hear it again. I pray you may never hear it.

We go to the mine silent in the morning, but we sing on the way home, glad to be coming to food and warmth and light and the laughter of women.

Now I have told you of my day. Will you tell me of yours?
With ever increasing devotion,
Owen

London
25 March 1876

Dear Owen,

I live in Kensington with my widowed aunt Elizabeth, my mother's sister, a delightful and spirited lady. She is considered a bit of a renegade in our family: she is a crusader for many causes, and even feels women should be allowed to vote. There are just three of us who live in the house: Aunt Elizabeth, Nora, who has been her housekeeper for twenty years, and I. This part of the city is like a little village unto itself, with its fishmonger, butcher, baker, fruiterer, and, of course, its ale-house.

It seems shameful to admit that I do not begin my day until ten in the morning when Nora comes to my room with tea and opens the shutters. By the time I come downstairs, my aunt is off to one of the meetings of societies that endlessly help the deserving poor. (I do not make light of poverty; there is too much of it in this city and in this country. However, might we not help people to earn both a living and some respect if we taught them a trade? There! My sermon is ended. My aunt teases me that I should be speaking in Hyde Park instead of on a stage.)

If the day is fair, I often walk in Kensington Gardens, the royal park near our home. (Our queen was born in the palace there, you know.) The spring flowers have been up for weeks now, as you told me they are in Llanelli, and forsythia is in bloom everywhere.

Afternoons, if there is no matinee performance, I take lessons—singing one day, piano another, elocution yet another. My speech teacher says I have a sibilant "s" and must conquer it if I am to succeed in my chosen profession.

Shortly after five o'clock, I arrive at the theater. More experienced actors arrive later, but I need much time to prepare myself. Oh, not my makeup. I need time to prepare my soul.

Yours,

Jessica

P.S. I have just read again your letter about a day in the mine. Your writing is impressive, as is your learning. When did you read Dante?

Llanelli
2 April 1876

Dearest Jessica,

We read Dante at the National School. We read Virgil, of course, in Latin, of course. And Shakespeare and Milton and Wordsworth. And our great Welsh epic, The Mabinogion, *even though we had to read it in English, not Welsh, as that language, alas, is not permitted at the school. Yet it is a language for bards.*

Do you know Mr. Matthew Arnold's poem "Lines Written in Kensington Gardens"? I read it, and thought of you.

Your aunt Elizabeth indeed sounds delightful and spirited. May I ask if your parents are well? I assume they are at too great a distance from London for you to live at home and travel to and from the theater.

Devotedly,
Owen

London
9 April 1876

Dear Owen,

My parents live here in London, in the house where I was born. My father is a much respected doctor. Sadly, when he saw that my love for the theater could not be confined to church pageants, he demanded that I give it up. I defied him, and he ordered me from the house. My mother had to choose between us, and I pray that one day I will understand her choice. My aunt defied them both to take me in.

Why am I telling you this? Perhaps because I want you to understand how much in my life I am willing to sacrifice for the theater.

Now I am almost sorry to have told you this, but I am going to post this letter before I think better of it.

Reluctantly,
Jessica

Llanelli
18 April 1876

Cariad,

I am sad for the rift between you and your parents, and sad for them, as well. And saddest for me, for what can I offer you for the loss you will suffer in coming to Llanelli?

Ah, Jessica, I can write you odes in Welsh and English, but they will not make up for ovations.

Forgive me. I can say no more today. Perhaps there is no more to say.

Owen

London
25 April 1876

Dear Owen, dear, dearest Owen,

You must write to me. I could not bear it otherwise. I wish I had not written my last letter to you, yet there must always be honesty between us.

Now I have not a shred of maidenly modesty remaining.

Your Jessica

Llanelli
2 May 1876

Cariad,

I care not a fig for maidenly modesty. I can only repeat the first words I ever spoke to you. Brava! Brava!

Your Owen

So they continued to write, and to reveal themselves to each other. Jessica, almost against her own will, began to fall more and more in love with him. Owen, busy building the house, wrote that his love grew "stronger with every beam, warmer with every thatch."

He worried, though, as he watched his mother at her chores, cooking and cleaning, boiling water in the great pot for the endless washdays that come with keeping a home for miners. He worried what the harshness of this life might do to Jessica. Suppose she would come to hate him for it? With a sigh, he wrote her that he was seriously thinking of becoming a teacher, not in Wales, but in London.

As she read that letter, Jessica asked herself if she could really be serious about this man. Am I mad even to think of it? she thought. What would I do in Llanelli? I would come to resent Owen for taking me away from the theater. And if Owen came to London, he could not realize his dream of owning a farm. Then she considered the most dreadful possibility of all. Suppose Owen left Wales because of her and came to hate her for it? Ah, she told herself, you must begin to prepare for the final curtain.

In June, their letters crossed. Owen wrote that the house was finished. Jessica wrote that a famous playwright had written a drama just for her. It was certain to make her a star if she could give the performance it deserved. She wanted Owen to know that she would shortly be very busy with readings; rehearsals would begin in October and the new play would open in London two weeks before Christmas.

As Jessica's letters grew fewer, Owen worked more furiously on the house in the glen. He whitewashed it. He built a table and four chairs. Built a bed and carved the headboard.

Carved a little cradle. When he could think of no more furniture to build, he whitewashed the house again.

In mid-October, Owen saw his mother waving at him to hurry as he walked up the hill with the men. They were singing their usual end-of-day chorus, but these days he seldom joined in. "A letter from London," his mother announced, breathless, waving it in the air. "Gwilym the Post made a trip on his bicycle so you would have it today."

"With enough stamps on it to ransom the crown jewels, and marked 'Rush' in three places," the postman added.

The men had stopped their singing. All eyes were on Owen. "From the queen, is it?" one of the men called out. "Are you called to sing before Her Majesty?" There was sympathetic laughter. Everyone in town knew what he had been building in the glen.

Owen opened the letter. He knew he had no possibility of going off by himself to read it. This was a public event in Llanelli. His father and brothers came out of the crowd of men, to stand with him if it was bad news. The letter was short. He read it silently, quickly, then read it again more slowly, making sure.

"Owen, my little one, what news?" his mother asked in the silence.

"The letter is from Miss Jessica Lavery, who is the star of a play that opens in London just before Christmas. She asks me to attend opening night as her guest."

The crowd cheered. His father and Branwen danced a little jig; his brothers shook his hand solemnly; the men sang a song of thanksgiving for tidings of joy.

His mother, he noticed, had tears in her eyes. Was she happy for him? Or sad to think she might be losing him to a wife? Or sad for some other reason only she could see?

Next day, in the dark of the mine, Owen thought only of Jessica. He wanted to give her a gift, and he could not afford pearls. A lovespoon was too homely. He decided he would carve an angel. An angel for the Christmas tree that would stand outside their home, where she could look up to God. He would carve her from the wood of a good Welsh plane tree, wood that would last for a thousand years. She would be the most beautiful angel in all the world, with a blue cloak, dark hair beneath a delicate gold crown, a sweet smile. And lavender eyes.

Two weeks before Christmas, Owen arrived at the theater

with the angel in his arms, wrapped in his mother's blue woolen shawl. The stage doorman eyed him with curiosity. "I've been doing this for thirty years, and never saw a leading lady who wanted a visitor just before the curtain goes up on opening night. Miss Lavery told me she won't see anybody else. But she wants to see *you*."

He led Owen to a dressing room with the name "Jessica Lavery" on the door, knocked, opened it, and stepped aside. Flowers were massed everywhere—in wreaths, in bowls, in vases, long-stemmed roses still in their moist boxes. Jessica was composed but pale beneath her makeup.

"Owen." Just the one word.

Again, all language deserted him. He had no English, no Welsh. He simply placed the package in her hands.

"A lovespoon?" She unwrapped the shawl, and the two pairs of lavender eyes met. "She's beautiful."

Owen looked around the dressing room. "You don't have a Christmas tree here?"

"No. Someone told me that the only place for a Christmas tree was outside, where—"

"Where it could look up to God," he finished for her. "Well, marry me and every year the angel will crown the tree we will have in front of our home." He paused, then continued, "In London."

Suddenly, she grew very stern. "I remember the tradition. If a woman accepts the carving, she accepts the man as her husband. But I must stay where my heart is, in the theater. And you must stay in Wales, where *your* heart is. And in the years to come, you will know this is the right decision."

"Never. Never, *cariad.*"

"*Cariad.* My beloved." She sobbed, and tried to hand the angel back to him, but his hands covered hers. They stood that way, the man holding the woman, the woman holding the angel, until a knock on the door broke the spell.

"Ten minutes, Miss Lavery," the stage manager announced.

"Now I *must* go." She looked for a last time into the angel's innocent face, thrust the figure to Owen, headed for the door, then stopped. "Good-bye." She said it quietly, without turning, with a deathly finality. And went out.

Owen knew the verdict was final. He bowed his head and cradled the angel in his rough hands. By some trick of light, he thought she looked sad.

The newspapers the next day reported that a star had been born to London theater. The critics praised the depth of the leading lady's performance, and her ability to capture the play's tragic quality. Rare in one so young, they agreed.

PART II

Christmas in Ashland, 1890

My great-grandmother Maggie Conyngham, like many young ladies in the nineteenth century, kept a journal. And, like many young ladies of her day, she knew that, without marriage, her future was rather bleak. She would be an "old maid schoolteacher," and try as she might, that seemed dreadful to her. I smile as I read her struggles, but I sympathize, because there *was no such thing as being a "career woman" in 1890 in Ashland, Pennsylvania.*

The following are excerpts from her journals of 1890 and 1891.

Monday, 20 October 1890

The year is almost over. It is time to take stock of myself.

Assets. I am well educated. I am well read. I am an English teacher at Miss Nightingale's respected Academy. I am attractive. (Really, Maggie, really and truly?) Well, my mirror tells me I am not beautiful, but I am not ugly either. My nose is a bit crooked, from that fall out of my crib, but it is not *disfiguring*. So why am I the only one of my friends, the only one of my classmates, not married? (Except for my fellow teacher Lucy Grunion, and although she is a lovely person, even she would have to admit that she is homely.)

I don't think I will ever love someone who will love me back; at least not at the same time. My attractions so far have been very one-sided. Everywhere around me, everyone is in *twos*—married couples, courting couples, old couples. I am the only *one*.

Not married at twenty-nine. I am an old maid school-teacher. (There! I wrote it as a fact. But it is a fact I cannot quite believe.)

I *must* stop thinking about marriage as women's only goal. I am getting worse than Mrs. Bennet in *Pride and Prejudice*.

Earlier this evening I attended the monthly meeting of the Ashland Ladies' Literary Society, and we discussed George Eliot's *Middlemarch*. Some of our members find it a painful tale, but I am much caught up in the lives of the characters. I should keep reading it tonight, as it is a long novel indeed, but I am weary.

And so, as Mr. Samuel Pepys always said, "and so to bed."

Monday, 27 October 1890

Lucy Grunion is a devotee of George Eliot and has been researching her life. She told me today in the teachers' room that Miss Eliot (or should I say Miss Evans, her real name) lived unwed with a gentleman for almost twenty-five years. Her family disowned her, but she stayed with him until he died. Would I have the courage to defy convention for love? Oh, I pray so.

Is it acceptable to pray for illicit outcomes?

Sunday, 2 November 1890

Yesterday afternoon a band from Harrisburg performed at the Lutheran church (the largest church in town), which was filled to overflowing. It was a stirring program. My favorite was "The Anvil Chorus," perhaps because the percussionists enjoyed it so much themselves.

Monday, 3 November 1890

Yesterday Mr. Rees, our minister, asked if I would have time for a word with him after services. It seems he is planning a Christmas pageant to be performed by the children on Christmas Eve, and he has asked *me* to take charge of it. He told me he has been impressed by my assistance of the choirmaster. I have no ear for music, and cannot sing, but I can make sure the members turn out for rehearsals and have the hymns in advance. Mr. Rees told me I was *well organized*. Is that a womanly virtue?

Friday evening, 7 November 1890

Henry Grunion comes to fetch his sister at school every Friday afternoon to drive her home to their parents' house for the weekend. Lucy told me recently that he thinks I am extremely intelligent. Today, he inquired after my health in a very interested way. But he has *limp fingers* when he shakes your hand. My father always said that the firmer a man's handshake, the stronger his character. And the name

Grunion reminds me of the witches in *Macbeth* talking about the "rump-fed runion." I looked that up in *Webster's* and couldn't find it, but it sounds disagreeable.

Saturday, 8 November 1890

We had the first meeting about our Christmas pageant. Parents brought the children who want to appear in our *tableaux vivants*. Goodness, there are many more volunteers than I expected. I had thought of staging three scenes: the Holy Family, the Three Kings and their retinue, and the shepherds, but I think we will have to add one with angels. All the children who can't be placed anywhere else will be angels.

Oh, dear. I'm afraid I will have to fashion a great many wings.

Saturday, 22 November 1890

Today we had our first rehearsal for the Christmas pageant. Many of the children I cast as shepherds want to be sheep. Their parents agree this is a charming idea. Oh, dear. I do not quite know how to costume for a sheep.

But I do love being part of something theatrical. (Even if it *is* in a church.)

There was a newspaper story this morning about the current census. I see I am in the official category denoted "Spinster."

Monday, 24 November 1890

The Literary Society finished our reading and discussion of *Middlemarch*. We were unanimous in approving of Dorothea for giving up a fortune in order to marry the man she truly loved. Well, *almost* unanimous. Lucy Grunion believes she should have lived with her lover unwed, just as the author did.

Monday, 1 December 1890

Mr. Kowalsky tipped his hat to me today when we passed in the street. He smiled and was pleasant, but I know I hurt his feelings when I declined to marry him two years ago. I had asked him if he liked reading poetry. He said: "I am proud to say I never read a poem in my life, and I don't plan to spoil the record now." And then he couldn't understand why I turned him down.

Saturday, 13 December 1890

Another long rehearsal today. As we waited for the mothers to come and pick up the children, one of the littlest sheep climbed into my lap and fell asleep. I put my arms around him and wondered if I would ever have a child of my own to put my arms around. It was such a fierce need that it shocked me. Would I go so far as to marry a man I did not truly love in order to have a family? Oh, I cannot imagine that.

Wednesday, 17 December 1890

My days have been full. There were final exams for the school term, which ends tomorrow, and papers to correct and return. Rehearsals for the Christmas performance. And all those costumes to make!

Some of the ladies at Miss Putnam's Residence volunteered to help me, so on many evenings we gather in the parlor to affix wings to the angels' robes and glue cotton batting to potato sacks for the sheep. Last evening Lucy Grunion brought a little volume of poetry by Miss Emily Dickinson, only recently published, and read to us while we sewed. I especially admire the poem about never seeing a moor or the sea, but knowing in your heart how they look.

Thursday, 18 December 1890

I woke up this morning to the good cinnamon smell of cookies baking. Miss Putnam is making Christmas cookies. She says it is a Pennsylvania Dutch tradition to bake enough to last until Easter. There are cookies everywhere, in cookie jars, on platters, on a three-tiered lazy Susan adorned with reindeer. Gingerbread men and women. Butter cookies in all sorts of shapes: Christmas trees with green sprinkles; bells with red sprinkles; tin soldiers with tiny silver candies for buttons. There are drop cookies made with oatmeal, and fancy cookies of white meringue or chocolate lace. There are snickerdoodles, baked with currants and walnuts. Another Pennsylvania Dutch tradition according to Miss Putnam, but she is not Pennsylvania Dutch and doesn't know where the name came from.

When I have a home of my own, I will bake cookies every Christmas. Enough to last until Easter. Oh, yes, and my children will help me bake them.

Christmas Eve, 1890

The *tableaux vivants* were a great hit. Balthazar wobbled a bit, and some of the sheep squirmed, but nobody seemed to mind. The Reverend Rees told me we had outdone the Lutherans, even if they do have a larger church.

Christmas Day, 1890

The Christmas service was beautiful and the music was splendid. There is a newcomer in the choir, quite a fine baritone, who sang a solo today. Lucy Grunion (who is in the choir) told me she thinks his name is Mr. Owens and that he has just come from the Mount Pleasant mine to work in the Ashland colliery. He reminds me of Heathcliff in *Wuthering Heights*. As though he could take on a moor. Or a sea.

There are only two of Miss Putnam's boarders in residence today: Miss Grimm and myself. So we were three, with Miss Putnam, for Christmas dinner. Miss Putnam carved our roasted chicken at the table, with a great clanging of knives, but she could not magic it into a turkey. We ladies ate our chicken silently, ate our plum pudding silently, murmured polite niceties about the dinner, and went to our rooms.

I have vowed that, when I am married, I will always roast a goose for Christmas. Just like the Cratchits in *A Christmas Carol*.

Monday, 5 January 1891

A new year. And a new semester. The girls in my class— fifteen and sixteen years of age—are just beginning to settle down after their holidays. There was much muffled giggling and talk of "and then he said" and choruses of "oh, no, did he really say that?" and I have to call them to order quite sternly and remind them that they are back in school and not at a cotillion. (Although I do not believe that anyone in Ashland, Pennsylvania, has ever heard of a cotillion, much less ever been to one.)

Mr. Blanchard, the art master here, came up to me at coffee hour in the teachers' room today and asked if I would give him some "instruction" in classical literature themes used by great artists. I told him I would be honored. But I will have to do some studying about it.

Wednesday, 14 January 1891

One month until Valentine's Day. I am remembering how silly I was just a year ago. I actually said a novena that I would receive a Valentine. When I was growing up, my Catholic girlfriends were always saying novenas to get things they wished for, and last February I went to Saint Anthony's nine mornings in a row, and prayed for a Valentine. I didn't get one, though. Maybe it doesn't work for Presbyterians.

It was silly, anyway.

Thursday, 29 January 1891

There was a terrible explosion Tuesday in the Mount Pleasant coal mine, in the west of Pennsylvania. More than a hundred miners were killed, some from the explosion itself, but most from a gas called "fire damp." The reports say that miners from all over the state are rushing there to offer aid. I wonder if men from our colliery are going. I wonder if Mr. Owens is going.

I will pray for them, and their poor families. How could a woman live every day with a man she loved going down into a mine?

Sunday, 8 February 1891

Today at church, Mr. Owens sang the solo, and he was quite . . . uplifting. As we were going out, I happened to be next to him so I told him how much I liked his singing, today and on Christmas. Well, he quite warmed up and told me that the Christmas song is an old Welsh hymn; in fact, that it is almost the "national anthem of Welsh hymns." I asked him how he knew that, and he looked at me in a surprised way and said that was, of course, because he was Welsh. And he told me that his name is Thomas, Owen Thomas.

Now that, I said to myself, is a nice name.

But he still reminds me of Heathcliff. There is something mysterious about him.

February 14

I have received no Valentines. My head aches and I do not feel like writing more.

Sunday, 15 February 1891

Mr. Thomas waited for me outside the church door this morning. When I came out, he tipped his hat and asked if he might escort me to my home.

"It is not really my home, sir. I reside at Miss Putnam's Residence for Refined Young Ladies."

He laughed at that. (It is a deep baritone laugh.) "Are *all* the ladies refined?"

"Quite refined, even though all the ladies are not young." I had not meant to say that; it slipped out. I felt my cheeks grow hot.

"If all the ladies are as lovely as you, Miss Putnam's must be a bower of beauty." My cheeks became even hotter. "You have a great advantage over me," he continued. "You know my name, but I do not know yours."

"Margaret Conyngham," I told him. "Spelled '*cony*' but pronounced like 'Cunningham.' They call me Maggie."

"Miss Conyngham." He nodded, and solemnly shook my hand. He escorted me to my door, and I watched from the parlor window as he walked away down the street. Owen

Thomas walked me home. Owen Thomas asked my name. Owen Thomas said I was lovely.

I *have* received a Valentine.

Sunday, 1 March 1891

Owen Thomas appeared at Miss Putnam's front door this morning as I was getting ready for church. He stood there with a bunch of vegetables in his hand.

"Do you know what today is?"

"Why, the first day of March."

"It is *Saint David's Day!*" he crowed. "The patron saint of the Welsh. And every man with a drop of Welsh blood wears a leek in his hat or a leek over his heart." He held the leeks up to me, like a bouquet. Then, with a flourish, he put on his cap, and I saw that it had a leek stuck through it.

"But I am not Welsh," I said.

"On Saint David's Day, *everyone* is Welsh," he answered, handed me the leeks, and sped off. They smell like onions, but it is a clean, earthy smell.

Thursday, 19 March 1891

Today in school we were reading Lord Tennyson's beautiful "Lady of Shalott." I suddenly found myself misty-eyed at the line: "She hath no loyal knight and true, the Lady of Shalott."

Owen tells me he likes to read poetry, and loves to hear it. Perhaps I will recite the whole poem to him next Sunday.

As I reread this entry, I see that I refer to him as Owen.

Monday, 23 March 1891

I *did* recite the Tennyson for Owen Thomas yesterday, and he applauded, then responded with a poem by Catullus, which he recited in *Latin*. The National School in Wales surely gave him a fine education.

Sunday, 5 April 1891

We have begun to settle into a routine, Mr. Thomas and I. A lovely routine. Every Sunday we meet after church and he escorts me home. Now that the weather is a bit warmer, we often sit on the front porch and talk for an hour or more, usually about literature.

Today was a special one, because he had invited me to Sunday dinner after the service. I expected we would dine at the tearoom, but he had made a reservation at the hotel dining room. It was quite grand. After we were seated, Mr.

Thomas asked me if I would care for a sherry, and I accepted. (My father had poured a tiny glass of sherry for me once, when our dog, dear shaggy Keeper, died of old age, and I was faint from grief. So I knew what sherry was, and did not much like it, but I wanted to appear worldly.)

The waiter reminded us sternly that it was a Sunday, and no liquor was served. We had both forgotten.

Mr. Thomas lifted a glass of water and toasted me. "Well, I owe you a glass of sherry, Maggie." My name sounded so natural coming from him that I just smiled and said, "Yes, Owen."

We ate creamed chicken in little pastry cups, very elegant, and drank endless cups of tea, and I asked him to tell me more about Wales. He told me more about the National School, which he attended until he was almost eighteen. He told me about studying the classics; of his love for Shakespeare and his special attraction to Wordsworth. "He and I both love sunshine and air and green growing things."

I asked him where he had lived—with his family or in a house of his own? For a moment his face grew dark, and I thought I had made him angry, but he brightened again. "I lived with my father—DaDa we called him, in the old Welsh way—and my good mother, and three brothers and a sister. I almost lived in my own house once, a house in a glen. But that did not happen."

And the look came over him again and I dared not ask another question.

Sunday, 12 April 1891

Today it was Owen who was full of questions. Where had I grown up? Where did my parents live now? Where had I attended school? Did I not consider myself remarkably well educated?

I told him that my mother and father died two years ago. They were visiting relatives in Johnstown and were drowned in the flood that swept over the city. "I am still very fearful of floods," I confessed. "Part of the reason I chose to teach in Ashland is because it is on high ground."

"And the other part of the reason?"

"Because they offered me the position," I said. He laughed his great laugh. And persisted in asking why my education was so "complete," as he termed it. I told him that my father taught theology at the University of Lewisburg, now called Bucknell University, and that I was in the first graduating class of the Women's Seminary there.

"Of course, our home was always a university. Almost every night, my father would read aloud to my mother and me—Shakespeare, Jane Austen, George Eliot, Dickens—and he would play all the parts. In different voices, at that."

"My father loved to read Dickens to us, too," Owen said. "And played all the parts, even the women."

"I love reading aloud. And playing parts," I told him.

"Do you? Do you indeed?" He looked grave, and took his leave.

Tuesday, 14 April 1891

It is after midnight, but I could not sleep, and so got up to write this in the half-dark. Owen came to call after dinner, which is unusual for him, because he must be at work in the colliery every morning at seven. He said he had been thinking about my delight in playing parts. Had I always wanted to become a teacher or did I have different ambitions? I told him I had once thought about becoming an actress. That strange shadow crossed his face again. "And why did you not pursue the theater?" he asked almost harshly.

"I felt my nose was not patrician enough," I confessed.

He laughed his wonderful laugh. "Oh, Maggie, your nose is beautiful. It gives you *character*. And just think, if you had gone on the stage, I might never have met you."

We talked so intently about so many things that neither of us realized it had become quite dark. Miss Putnam had to pop her head out to remind us that it was after nine o'clock.

Sunday, 17 May 1891

For the first time, I brought up the Mount Pleasant mine disaster, and asked Owen if he were ever afraid, working down there. He told me he was afraid every day of his life. He said: "I told someone once that a mine is a hellish place, but now I think I was wrong. It is more like Dante's Purgatory, because there is a possible escape, unlikely as it is, which makes the punishment even harder to bear. And God is very far away."

Thursday, 11 June 1891

A touring company from Philadelphia is coming to Mahanoy City to present Shakespeare's *Twelfth Night*, and Owen has invited me to attend the matinee performance. It is my favorite Shakespearean play. No, it is my favorite play of all!

As I look back over my journal entries these past months, they are full of "Mr. Thomas" this and "Mr. Thomas" that, and "Owen," "Owen," "Owen." At this rate I will need *two* journals before the year is out.

Saturday, 27 June 1891

Twelfth Night was glorious—at once funny and romantic and beautiful. The actress who played Viola/Sebastian is a young woman with cascades of golden hair and large brown eyes. She spoke her lines with great intelligence and feeling. When the curtain fell, I stood and applauded until my hands ached. "Oh, Owen," I begged, "let's go to the stage door and wait for her to come out so we can tell her that she was marvelous!"

"No!" Owen said in a strangled voice, so sharply that I jumped. "We must be getting back to Ashland. And I don't like hanging about stage doors making a nuisance of myself."

There was that look of his again. So now, in addition to his reminding me of Heathcliff, he makes me think of Jane Eyre's Mr. Rochester. A man who harbors a deep secret.

Saturday, 4 July 1891

Owen and I went to the Ashland Independence Day celebration this morning. The mayor spoke, although it was hard to hear him due to the noise, with all the boys exploding their firecrackers or shooting blank cartridges. The parade was grand. The high school band played a patriotic medley, the Scottish pipers came from Kulpmont and marched in their kilts, the volunteer firemen rode in their newly shined red truck. The crowd cheered as the veterans of the War Between the States marched past, each waving a flag.

I asked Owen if all this American patriotism made him uncomfortable. "Why, Maggie," he said, surprised. "Did you not guess? I *am* an American. I became a citizen three years ago." And he waved his own flag under my nose. "An American you are wanting, is it? An American you have." I smiled to myself, because he had never sounded more Welsh.

Saturday, 15 August 1891

We drove in Owen's buggy to the other side of the mountain, where the slag heaps are hidden from view, and Owen selected a pretty meadow near a stream. I opened the picnic basket and put the dishes out on a flat rock in the sun. We had deviled ham sandwiches and lemonade; Owen pronounced both excellent. After our little lunch, we picked daisies, and Owen put them together with some ferns and gave them to me as a bouquet.

They are in water now, here in my room. As much as I wanted to try "He loves me, he loves me not," I was too afraid to do so. I will press one in my Bible instead. In the Song of Solomon.

Saturday, 22 August 1891

Today is my thirtieth birthday. I have nothing else to write.

Monday, 7 September 1891

The first day of school! I made sure to arrive early so I could stand outside to greet any of my returning students. My friend Lucy Grunion drove up with her brother; she jumped out, kissed me, and told me she had missed me terribly all summer long. Mr. Grunion got down from the buggy to shake my hand and ask if I had enjoyed a pleasant vacation. He still has *limp fingers.*

As he drove off, another buggy drew up. It was Mr. Blanchard, the art master, with a plump lady on the seat next to him. "Oh, Miss Conyingham, Miss Grunion. May I present my wife, Mrs. Blanchard."

Suddenly, everyone seems to be in *twos* again.

Sunday, 13 September 1891

The annual hayride was announced in church today; it will be three weeks from yesterday. This is an important event, because it has become accepted custom here at our church that when a gentleman asks a young lady if he may escort her to the hayride, it is a public acknowledgment of his special affection for her. The deacon reading the announcements noted that there would be a full moon for the occasion, and some of the girls giggled.

Owen was waiting at the door as usual, and we strolled home. More slowly than usual, I thought, as I waited for him to ask me to the hayride. When we reach the next bush he will ask me. At the white gate, he will ask me. On the pathway to the house, he will ask me.

He did not ask me.

By the time we reached the porch I was close to tears. Not because of the hayride, but because I had so misjudged Owen's feelings for me.

"You are looking pensive, Maggie. No, looking sad."

I could not help myself. "I am sad because you did not ask me to the hayride."

He looked puzzled. "The hayride? Ask you to the hayride?" Then his face cleared. "Ah, I did not *ask* you to the hayride because I assumed . . . I felt you knew . . . that of course we would . . ." He stopped, took a long breath, and plunged in again. "I assumed you know that I care for you. And hope that you care for me. But perhaps I have assumed too much."

I turned from the door. "Oh, you assumed exactly right, Owen Thomas. I do care for you. I care for you very much."

And right there, on Miss Putnam's porch, in broad daylight, I threw my arms around him and kissed him.

Saturday, 3 October 1891

Owen Thomas has asked me to marry him and I have accepted.

Last evening he came straight from the mine to Miss Putnam's, dirty and smudged as he was with coal dust, to ask if I would mind *not* going on the hayride today. I asked with some concern if he was feeling ill. He replied that he was in the best of health, but begged some time to be alone with me. He had an important question to ask. My heart fluttered.

This afternoon he came for me in his buggy, and took me to the meadow where we had our picnic last August. "This is the spot in Ashland that most reminds me of Llanelli," he said. "So this is where I wanted to be with you today." Then he was silent for a long time, and there was no sound but the brook and the birds. "Maggie, I had planned to recite some lines from *Epithalamion*, but they have deserted me. Right now, I cannot even remember more of Sonnet 116 than 'Let me not to the marriage of true minds admit impediments.' So. To my question. Will you marry me, Maggie?"

"Yes," I said. "Yes, oh yes, oh yes. I was awake half the night praying this was the question you were planning to ask."

He laughed with delight. "The thing I love most about you, Maggie, is your honesty. No, there is one thing I love more."

"What is that?" I asked.

"Your nose," he said.

Monday, 5 October 1891

After church yesterday, we sat on the glider on Miss Putnam's porch for so many hours that she came out to ask if we were not afraid of catching a chill. That was her way of telling us we were becoming a bit "conspicuous." When we told her of our engagement, she invited us into her parlor for a glass of elderberry wine. She makes it herself. Imagine.

Owen and I are to be married in the spring. Oh, I wish my mother were here. I wish she could put the bridal veil on my head and sit in the first pew and cry, as I know she would. I wish my father could walk down the aisle and give me away.

Goodness! Who *will* give me away?

Suddenly, it seems as though years have passed since I hoped Owen would ask me to the hayride.

Wednesday, 4 November 1891

I have not written in weeks. I did not know that being a bride would take so much time. As the news spread (the news of our betrothal, that is), the teachers held a tea for me, and my fellow boarders at Miss Putnam's held a breakfast.

I have reserved the church. And of course Mr. Rees with it.

I have asked Lucy Grunion to be my maid of honor. She immediately made me promise I would throw the bridal bouquet straight into her hands. She reminds me of myself before I met Owen.

Owen. I write his name with such love attached to each letter. He told me his friends in the mine gave him three cheers on his engagement, and then they all went back to work as usual. Men do not have the stress of marriage planning that women do.

Dear Journal, I wonder if I will keep writing these entries after we are married. It suddenly occurs to me that Owen does not know I keep a journal. Not that it is anything to hide, but I hope we will have no secrets from each other.

Sunday, 15 November 1891

Owen is distracted. I think he is worried about something. Today, he walked me home from church as always, then left immediately, saying he had some paperwork to do.

Tuesday, 24 November 1891

My hand is shaking so that I can hardly write.

Owen came to see me unexpectedly, late this afternoon, dressed in his black Sunday suit, to tell me he had just signed the final papers to buy a small farm about fifty miles from here. He told me that has been his dream for many years; that he had come to America to work in the mine until he saved enough money for the farm. It is a small farm with a small house on it, he told me, and it would become his in exactly thirty days, on December 24. On Christmas Eve.

"I want to take you home to my house, Maggie. To *our* house. Will you marry me on Christmas Eve, Maggie, and go with me?"

I wanted to say to him: "Whither thou goest I will go, and where thou lodgest I will lodge." But all I could say was "Yes, Owen." I had no regrets at all about the church wedding and the white gown, but the mind is a curious thing. All I could think about was Lucy Grunion and how sadly she will miss catching the bridal bouquet.

Later I asked Owen about his decision to leave mining. "Do you remember the Tennyson poem you recited to me? The Lady of Shalott says, 'I am half sick of shadows.' Well, I have done with shadows. I have done with mines. I will never live in the dark again."

Wednesday, 25 November 1891

Owen has opened his heart to me. His heart and his past. And, I believe, his soul.

It was very painful for him. For both of us.

He told me there is a centuries-long tradition in Wales that every good man must pay his debts and right his wrongs before the New Year. And he told me he owed me the debt of honesty. He had been in love with a beautiful English actress. The newspapers called her "the girl with the lavender eyes." Owen was so sure they would be married that he had built a little home for them in Wales; he even carved an angel for their Christmas tree.

I waited for the axe to fall. That he is still in love with her.

"But it was not to be. I would have left Wales for her, left the land and gone to London, but Jessica would not permit that."

"And is she still on the stage in London?" I asked him, almost in a whisper.

"She is. She has fulfilled her dream of becoming one of the great actresses of our time."

We were silent, just standing there facing each other. My thoughts tumbled over each other and I closed my eyes and cobbled together a silent little prayer. "Dear God, let me not ask him if he still loves her. If I do not ask, he will not have to answer. And I will be content to live with him for the rest of my life even if he does not love me." But the words escaped from me. "Do you love her still?"

"Open your eyes and look at me, Maggie," Owen said. "I *did* love her, but that is in the past. Now you help fulfill a dream for me, of marriage, of owning a farm, of a home in a glen, with a fireplace and a nursery." He took my hand. "I love *you*, Maggie. I love you very much."

Christmas Eve, 1891

Reverend Rees married us this morning in his study.

I wanted to record every word that was said, every minute of the ceremony, but now I can't remember a thing. We set off for the farm right afterward in Owen's buggy. It was cold, although not windy, and he threw a great heavy blanket over me, and tucked it around me, and we were off. I thought he would kiss me as he swaddled me, but he did not.

We drove for more than five hours. I was half asleep

when Owen announced: "We are here."
Even though it was almost dark, I could
see that the house had whitewashed
walls, like the houses in Wales he had
described to me. And there was the
sound of a stream.

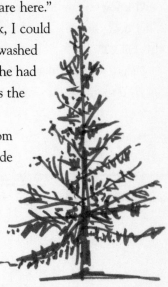

Owen helped me down from
the buggy. "The tree right beside
the door is a blue spruce,
Maggie, and every year from
now on we will decorate it
at Christmastime, here,
outside, where it can look
up to God." He handed me
a knobby bundle. "This is our first decoration."

I undid the wrapping, a woman's blue woolen shawl, and
looked at the wooden angel. Owen held a lantern up so I
could see her. "She has lavender eyes," I said. And I could add,
and mean it: "She is beautiful."

"And now she is yours," Owen said.

"Now she is ours, and we will place her on our tree
together." I held out my hand to him and he led me toward
the house. Suddenly I laughed with surprise.

"What is it?" Owen asked.

"I know we are in Pennsylvania, I know this is our home, but I don't know where I am," I said. "What is the name of this place?"

"It is called Bethlehem," my husband told me.

And then the stars came out.

PART III

Christmas in No-Man's-Land, 1917

Maggie and Owen had four children, three sons and one daughter. This part of the story is about James, the middle son: my grandfather, born in 1895. James Thomas was a contradiction in terms: a pacifist pugilist. At least he was until he *woke up in a London hospital on Christmas Eve, 1917, without most of the muscles in his left leg.*

"Move the ladder a little over to the right. I can't reach the top of the tree." It was a man's voice, deep enough to be my father's, but different. "Let me get on up there. I'm taller." A softer voice, younger, but not one of my brothers. I opened my eyes and a Christmas tree came into focus, and two men in bathrobes, putting ornaments on it. "We need to move the ladder," one repeated. I closed my eyes again. My leg was throbbing and I felt faint.

"You're nine years old now, James," my mother said, *"so this year you shall have the honor of putting the angel on the top of the tree."*

"He's not tall enough, Mama," my big brother David objected. *"I was taller than James when I was nine. Taller than him when I was seven."*

"Taller than he," Mama corrected automatically. *She had been a schoolteacher and never let us forget it.*

"I'm as tall as him now and I'm only seven." My little brother, Thomas.

"As tall as he," Mama sighed.

"When do I get to put the angel on the tree?" That from

my little sister, Susie. She asked the same question every year.

And every year my mother gave her the same answer. "Girls don't climb ladders."

My father put his arm around me and urged me toward the ladder leaning against the tree. I climbed up a few rungs and turned. "Why can't we have a tree inside like everybody else?"

"Hush," Mama said. My father handed the angel to me. Only by climbing to the very highest rung and standing on my tiptoes could I place the angel at the top. The group below applauded, as they did every year. I climbed back down and saw that my father had been steadying the ladder. "I still don't understand why we can't have a tree that's—"

"Because it's a tradition, and God knows there are few enough around these days, so when a family has a good one, they should cherish it." He patted my shoulder. "Well done, James."

"Thank you, DaDa." I was the only one of his sons who sometimes used that old Welsh term for father, but he liked it, and it made our relationship a special one in my eyes. My hands were cold beneath my mittens; my toes were cold inside my boots. I looked up at the angel and said quietly to myself, But I wish we had a Christmas tree inside like other people.

I opened my eyes and looked straight up into a crystal chandelier. "Where am I?" There was no answer. I asked again, and realized my mouth was so dry that I hadn't uttered a sound. I tried to sit up but couldn't and fell back against the pillow.

"Have a little water." A man's deep voice. The water tasted wonderful, the best thing I had ever drunk in my life. "Where am I?"

"You're in No-Man's-Land." A younger voice, laughing.

"Don't scare the lad," said the man holding the water glass. His face began to come into focus. "You're in the American Women's War Relief Hospital in Belgravia. When they brought you in yesterday, they said you were wounded in the Zeppelin raid on Piccadilly Circus. But you're going to be okay. Nasty leg, but you'll walk."

"Are you the doctor?"

He stood up beside my bed, and I saw he wore a bathrobe and a hospital gown. "I'm just a patient."

The younger voice broke in again. "Don't look for too many doctors in this ward. Or nurses. The American nurses came over here to take care of the British wounded, and they don't want to show favoritism to us. The British doctors take care of their own first. That's why we call this ward No-Man's-

Land. You're between two fronts here. Basically on your own."

I raised my head enough to see he was just one bed away. "I'm Eli, Eli Scruggs, from the great state of Virginia, where we are raised with the good manners to introduce ourselves. Unlike certain Vermonters."

The patient beside my bed grinned and held out his hand. "Shank. Sergeant Ed Shank from Putney, Vermont. Have some more water."

The word triggered a memory.

"The water is rising awfully fast." My mother's voice was shaky. *"It's getting so close to the house."*

"Maggie, we've had this conversation every year when the spring thaw sets in, and I'm sure we'll have it every year for the rest of our lives. The worst we've ever had, from the day we arrived here, is a trickle of water in the basement." My father tried to sound comforting, but there was an edge of exasperation. He needed to get back out to the fields.

"You go on, DaDa. You and Davey and Tom can start plowing. I'll stay here with Mama, chop some wood and keep an eye on the water in that run." I knew that flooding terrified Mama, but she had good reason. Both her parents had drowned in the terrible Johnstown Flood.

"There's a good lad you are, James." In moments of excitement, he always reverted to Welshness. *A clatter, a scuffle of boots and*

boys and dogs and doors banging shut, and my mother and I were alone. She was still standing at the window.

"Thank you, Jamie, my little one." She had picked that Welsh expression up from my father, who used "my little one" affectionately to address everything from babies to bulls. I was indeed her little one, in fact; my brothers had several inches on me and said I was the runt of the litter.

Mama came away from the window and checked the fire in her scary big black coal stove, which never went out. When I read a book about a princess and goblins a couple of years ago, I thought the goblins lived inside that stove.

As she often did, my mother jumped right inside my thoughts. "You take after me in all sorts of ways. You're my bookworm, and I'm proud of you for that." I thought of some of the books my mother had read to me or taken out of the library; how did she, a girl, know so much about what boys would like? Graustark and Castle Craneycrow. Kidnapped and Treasure Island and Ivanhoe.

"You and I like adventure," she continued, *"but it has to be a courtly kind of adventure. No violence. No cruelty."* It was true. Neither one of us could abide hog butchering time. Mama took the buggy into town on some pretext or other. I took a book and walked miles and miles away from the farm, and stayed away until dark. My brothers teased me, but I was resolute.

"Thomas! Thomas! You've been asleep again and we didn't want you to miss out on Christmas Eve dinner. It's chicken." It was my friend from Vermont. "And besides, they tell us one of the doctors is coming any minute."

"Because there's a Limey in this ward." I began to realize that Eli and Ed did a kind of vaudeville routine, swatting back and forth, enjoying every moment. "He's by way of being our hero. Seaforth Highlanders."

"They brought him here after his surgery when the other wards were full and now they don't want to risk moving him." Ed lowered his voice. "They're not sure if he'll lose the arm."

"He's a laugh a minute," Eli Scruggs said loudly. "Keeps us all in stitches, don't you, Scotty? After they turn you out of here, you going back to the front?"

The big Highlander was lying flat in his bed, most of him covered in plaster, but his voice was clear despite the burr. "I don't want to be like those swanks who say they *want* to. I'd rather not. But I'll go back if I have to. I'm no pacifist."

"I'm glad you've decided to be a pacifist," my mother said. "You're fourteen years old and a good, God-fearing boy."

"God has nothing to do with it," I told her with terrible seriousness. "I am an ethical pacifist."

"I don't know what that is," Mama objected. "And I've been wondering about you and God. Sometimes at church, you have the same look on your face as you do when we're entertaining guests who don't particularly interest you. You are polite and say all the right things, but somehow your heart isn't in it."

"I go to church with you every single Sunday."

"It isn't the going, Jamie. It's the believing I'm not sure about with you. You help decorate the big tree every single Christmas, and help put the angel on it, but I don't think you believe in it."

"My way to God seems dark, Mama."

"But when you believe, James, the way is suddenly full of light. And the world becomes happy, too. As happy as . . . as a Christmas tree with an angel at the top."

"Cheerio, all," said the nurse. I could tell from her accent that she was American. Not my type; almost as tall as I am, skinny. Fidgety. She was making her way around the ward, handing out little boxes of chocolates and cigarettes. She seemed to be in a hurry to leave, I thought; she hadn't bothered to take off her cape. She stopped at my bed. "Merry Christmas. You're the new patient. They told me you were hit in the Zeppelin raid yesterday. You know, you were the only American casualty. Bad luck. All the others were British. All civilians."

"Civilians?" I echoed.

"Yes. But only nine of them were killed. Get better fast. Ta, as we say over here." She was off to finish her distribution, eager no doubt to get back to her British patients.

Nine. What was it she said? *Only* nine.

"Happy Christmas," said the British doctor, unrolling the bandages to look at my leg. "You were the only American, you know. Rotten luck." He peered at my leg. "All told, I think we've done a splendid job. But the main credit goes to you, your constitution. You'll always have a bit of a limp, but you'll handle it just fine. You're a tough one."

"You're a tough one," the Bucknell boxing coach said. It was my freshman year, and everybody was surprised when I took up the sport. There I was, the pacifist, the family peacemaker, punching people in the gut and whenever possible on the chin. I loved it.

First of all, I loved Bucknell. My mother went there; of course it was the Women's Seminary when she attended, but the same spirit prevailed. And my maternal grandfather taught theology there. So with this sort of double legacy and a good high school record, I won a generous scholarship. That, plus a stipend earned by waiting on tables in the men's dining room, got me through. When I joined the Phi Gamma Delta fraternity after rush, I didn't feel at all like some poor boy from a farm.

"So, Toughy," the coach continued, "if you do everything I tell you to do, and don't ask questions, and train hard, you'll be a good boxer. You may even be a champ." I worshipped him.

My mother came to just one fight, early in my Bucknell career. I won, but my opponent managed to give me a bloody nose. Mama almost fainted. When I came home at spring break she sat me down. "I want to have a serious talk with you about this fighting."

"It's boxing, Mama."

"It's about hitting people. And you a pacifist."

"I would never hit anyone in anger."

"But are you sure it's a sport for gentlemen?"

"Theodore Roosevelt thought so, Mama." I had just finished reading his autobiography, published the year before, 1913. TR became my role model, for studying hard, training hard, preparing myself for important things. TR boxed at Harvard; I would box at Bucknell.

I became middleweight champion of the university in my junior year and held the title until I graduated. My fraternity brothers had learned my nickname from the coach, and sometimes the

crowd would chant it at a match. Toughy. Toughy. Toughy. I
quite liked being Toughy Thomas. My brothers, both taller, began
to look up to me.

"Well, Merry Christmas Eve, all!" Ed Shank had decided
to eat dinner at my bedside. His plate was on his lap, mine on
a bed tray. Because I was still considered "recently wounded,"
I was allowed only broth, gelatin pudding, and tea. Ed cut
into his chicken. "Oh, God, this is one really old hen."

"Remember there's a war on here," Eli commented from
his bed. He took another drag on his cigarette. He wasn't
eating.

"Don't you like chicken?" I asked him.

"Sure, but I'm Roman Catholic. Christmas Eve is a fast day
for us. No meat at all. Back home, Ma would always make a
vegetable stew; we called it 'Amen Stew.' It wasn't bad, except
for the okra. Damn slimy vegetable, okra."

"I've never had okra." Eli signed that I was lucky. "And you
couldn't eat even a little chicken leg?" I think there were a
couple of Catholics at Bucknell, but I never actually sat down
and *ate* with one. Suddenly, Eli Scruggs seemed wonderfully
exotic. "Would you go straight to Hell?"

"Hell, I don't know. But for sure my pa would take me out
to the woodshed."

Ed grunted. "Well, I'm sorry, but I wouldn't last long with any religion that told me I couldn't have meat with my potatoes."

"How long have you been in the army, Eli? Ed?" I wanted to change the subject.

Ed was the first to answer. "Well, let's see. The United States declared war in April. And, just like every American male between twenty-one and thirty-five, I received a draft notice in May. Signed up in June. And before I really knew which end of a gun was which, I was in France. And then bang! I was here."

"This is a pretty grand hospital, isn't it?"

"It's a palace! Home of Lady Caroline something. All over England, they're turning their mansions over to the government to make them into hospitals. Just last week, the Duchess of Marlborough and Lady Randolph Churchill were here, visiting. She's a stunner, that Lady Randy. But how about you, James? Did you get drafted, too?"

"I expect I'll be drafted soon, DaDa. But I think I'm going to register as a CO—a conscientious objector."

"That's a serious decision, son. Not one to be made lightly."

"Oh, I've thought about it. I could still see action, you know, be right there at the front, as an ambulance driver or a litter bearer. But I wouldn't have to shoot anybody. Kill anybody."

"The Germans aren't just anybody, James. From what I read, they are killing a lot of women and children. And the way I interpret the Bible, it is right and just to kill your enemies in self-defense."

"I'm not a religious pacifist, DaDa. I'm an ethical pacifist. I believe in peace. That's what I'm for."

"And I'm for bed," Mama said, and put a pot of coffee on the table between us. "And my prayers will be that whether it is God or whether it is ethics, you will make the decision that feels right to you."

My father and I talked until it was almost morning. Then he went out to begin the usual farm day, and I went out to tramp the woods beside the run. At mid-morning I drove the old Ford truck into Bethlehem. A few hours later, when I pulled up beside the house, my father came out of the barn and my mother came to the kitchen door. They knew from the look on my face what I had decided to do.

"I wasn't drafted, Ed," I said. "I enlisted as an ambulance driver."

The orderly turned off most of the lights in the ward, leaving just a few on for the night nurse to see her way around. I lay in bed, smoking and looking at the Christmas tree and thinking about my bad luck. It wasn't a *real* Christmas tree without an angel. And it wasn't a real Christmas. It was a lousy Christmas. Why did I have the bad luck to get a three-day pass? Why did I have the bad luck to decide to come to London? The bad luck to want to be in Piccadilly?

"They tell me you are one lucky fellow." Even in the dim light I could tell this nurse was pretty. She leaned over my bed, put a thermometer in my mouth, and took off her cape. She was slim, but not one of those scrawny ones.

"I'll probably have a limp the rest of my life."

She waved it away. "What's a little limp between friends? And don't talk with the thermometer in your mouth."

She was another of the American nurses, but there was a softness to her consonants I couldn't quite place. Obediently, I stayed silent until she read my temperature, then held out my hand. "James Thomas. Pennsylvania."

"I know who you are. I'm Katie O'Gara. Virginia."

"Ah, the wrong side. But we Celts have to stick together." We shook hands and I couldn't help adding: "Even if you are a Rebel. But how on earth did you get *here*?"

Katie grinned. "By ship. An American troop ship, as a matter of fact."

I grinned back. Celts together. "You know what I meant. I see from your cap you're a full-fledged RN."

"That's exactly why I'm here. I graduated from nursing school in June, and when we came into the war, I decided to come over and help."

"Are you sure which side you're on, Johnny Reb?" I teased.

"Now don't you be asking me about slavery and states' rights and all that." She was very stern.

"I wasn't going to mention that."

"But you were *thinking* it."

I admitted she was right. I *was*. "But we have to form a unified front here. You're Irish, I'm Welsh. What part of Ireland?"

"My folks are from the *north*. So please don't be asking me about shamrocks and bogs and leprechauns, Mr. Thomas."

"I was going to ask no such thing." Miss O'Gara would have done okay on the Bucknell boxing team.

"But you were—"

"Thinking it." We completed the sentence together. She laughed, a great deep draught that reminded me of the way my father laughed. There was none of a girl's giggly, chirpy tone.

She plumped my pillow, straightened my blanket, adjusted her uniform. "And you are making me forget I have fourteen other patients on this ward, Mr. Thomas, with your Celts and your states' rights and your leprechauns!"

I watched her as she checked the patient in the next bed,

and then moved on to Eli Scruggs. She gave him a package, a sort of lump wrapped in wax paper. Even though I knew I was snooping, I sat up to see what he unwrapped. A Christmas present? The greasy paper came away. She had brought Eli Scruggs fish-and-chips for his holiday dinner.

My father, as always, carved the Christmas leg of lamb. (He called it a "joint," in the English way.) He delivered perfectly symmetrical slices, all of uniform thickness, to the big white platter. "Pennsylvania lamb is good, but not as good as Welsh mutton, which is the best in the world," he declared, as he did every Christmas since I could remember. Tom and I grinned at each other as he began the sentence, and mouthed the ending together.

"We learned in school that lambs are sheeps." Little Susie was the family know-it-all. "And sheeps come from Texas."

"Sheep," my mother corrected automatically. "It's always singular. And you boys"—this to Tom and me; she hadn't missed our pantomime—"you mind your manners. Eat your meat and vegetables, or no pudding for dessert."

"You fell asleep and didn't even eat your pudding." Katie O'Gara was back beside my bed. "It's almost midnight. Will you be able to go to sleep again?"

"Not yet." I patted the bed. "Sit down and talk to me for a while."

"Oh, nurses aren't allowed to sit down. Not ever while we're on duty. And especially not on patients' beds. The matron would faint. But the ward is quiet so I can stay here with you for a few minutes. Tell me how you happened to be right there in Piccadilly Circus when the Zeppelin dropped the bomb. The only American. Mr. Thomas, you need not do another thing in this war. You are already unique."

I told her about enlisting as an ambulance driver in June, and being sent to England, to training at a camp north of London, my joy at receiving a three-day Christmas pass that allowed me to come to the city. As I babbled on, I realized that it had been months since I had a receptive female listener. "And I decided to see every inch of London, starting with Piccadilly. So there I was. And here I am. In a hospital that takes care of the gallant British wounded, and ignores us trashy Americans." I hadn't meant to say that, but I felt it.

Have you ever seen a person actually get her Irish up? That's what Katie did, standing there beside my bed. Her cheeks turned pink, and her voice dropped about an octave. "Don't you dare say that! Don't you just dare! The British have been fighting off the Germans for three years, while America had *debates*. They were dying, while we *talked*." Most girls get all squeaky when they're excited. I liked that she didn't.

"Let me give you a little education about pacifism, Miss

O'Gara. America was concerned about the ethics of going to war. If you would read Mr. Eugene Debs, he says—"

"I *have* read Mr. Eugene Debs. He is not against war because of killing. His opposition is that the master class declares the war, and the subject class fights it."

I had to admit she was right, but I struggled on. "Miss Helen Keller is most persuasive about pacifism. She believes—"

Katie flashed forth again. "Miss Helen Keller is an extraordinary woman, and I admire her greatly. But she believes America is invincible, that no country, including Germany or Japan, would dare to attack us. And I think she is wrong." Her cheeks grew pinker.

"Well, the best arguments come from Mr. Mohandas Gandhi in India, who teaches the power of nonviolence."

She was just as fast in submission as she was in disagreement. "I have not read Mr. Gandhi, but now I will."

Well, I thought, thank God there's *somebody* I've read that she hasn't. Aloud I said only, "Thank you."

"The British are doing everything they can to make us welcome. Do you see that tapestry on the wall? It's a Gobelin. Priceless. *Priceless!* But Lady Caroline said it should remain in place, to make it seem more like a home here, and less like a hospital."

I squinted at the tapestry. Gobelin? Had I heard that name before? Maybe during the art history course I took.

Katie plunged on, determined to make me appreciate British hospitality. "They even put up a Christmas tree in every ward."

"Did you have a Christmas tree at home in Virginia?"

"We are not barbarians in Virginia," she flared, then relented. "We have special Christmas traditions like the Yule log, which is lighted on Christmas Eve and not allowed to go out until Twelfth Night. We throw sprigs of holly onto the fire, to represent all the troubles of the past year that are not to return again. Oh, Christmas is an *elegant* season, when we polish up the silver tea service. We have eggnogs. *Everyone* drinks eggnogs, even the ladies. My father makes them with rum *and* sherry." Her face was soft, remembering. "Oh, and champagne. We always had champagne with Christmas dinner. What are your Yankee traditions?"

"They are really more Thomas family traditions. Our Christmas dinner, for example. My father, the Welshman, insists that only leg of lamb will do, even though it is not as tasty as Welsh mutton. My mother, the literary one, insists we have roast goose like the Cratchits in *A Christmas Carol*. So we have both. It makes Christmas a bit indigestible, but my parents are happy." Katie and I laughed together. It was a nice moment.

And then I told her about the angel my father had carved years ago, the angel with lavender eyes who was always at the top of the tree, that stood outside where it could look up to God.

Katie was misty-eyed. "What a beautiful tradition. I will take that home with me." Then she grew stern again. "Now I want you to drink this. It will help you sleep." It tasted bitter, but in a pleasantly bitter way.

"I'm not ready to go to sleep."

"Try. Think of pleasant things. Think of Christmases at home."

Christmases at home. I watched Katie start her rounds, listened to the bells striking midnight, looked again at the tapestry. It was hard to make out the scene, but I thought the figure was a shepherdess. Wasn't a shepherdess sort of like a nurse, always caring for her charges? I looked again at the Christmas tree. There was nothing at the top, and, once again, I missed the angel. Katie would be finished with her rounds in another hour; I decided to stay awake until she could come back to talk with me.

✳

"Good morning! Merry Christmas!" The draperies had been pulled back from the big windows, and pale light was coming in; it couldn't quite be called sunshine. I realized I was hungry. "Merry Christmas, James," Eli said again. "You had a good sleep, and I will swear to any girlfriend you bring around that you don't snore. Just an occasional snort. And look at your breakfast tray; you're allowed to eat today. Bangers and beans."

"And don't forget to pull your Christmas cracker," the American nurse chimed in. She was the tall, skinny one from yesterday.

"What the hell is a Christmas cracker?" This from Ed, his mouth full of sausage.

"Don't swear in front of me, especially on Christmas Day," she mock-scolded. "Christmas crackers are a grand old English tradition."

"Not so old actually." Scotty was the only one of us being fed by an orderly, because both his arms were immobilized. "Invented quite recently, not grand and old like *Scots* traditions. It's just a cardboard cylinder to hold a wee gift and a paper hat. You pull the little string at both ends, and it gives a bang." He nodded encouragement to the orderly, who pulled obediently. It gave a listless pop, and the wrappings fell away. "Each person puts on a paper hat, so each is a king or a queen for Christmas."

"Are Scottish Christmas traditions very different from the British?" I was curious.

"Oh, aye, but even more so are the customs for the new year. It's considered good luck if the first person who enters your home after midnight on the first day of the year is a dark man."

"Why must he be dark?"

"The Vikings pillaged the Scottish coast for years, and they were all fair-complexioned. The Scots are dark. So a dark man entering your home would be a kinsman, a friend. A good way to start the year." Scotty grinned. "Or it could just be Celtic superstition."

Celtic. The American nurse passed near my bed. "Nurse," I called urgently.

"Miss Rogers. Do you need something?"

"Oh, no," I said. "Do you know when Miss O'Gara will be back on duty?"

"Miss O'Gara." She frowned. "I don't know any Miss O'Gara. Nurses keep coming in all the time, you know. Coming in and going out. I can't keep up with them all."

It was hours before the British doctor came into the ward. He was even more in a hurry than yesterday, and I could smell the whiskey on his breath. He glanced at the bandages on my leg. "No temperature. No infection. I'm not going to change these dressings today. We'll let that leg alone for a day or two."

"Do you know an American nurse here, a Miss Katie O'Gara?"

"O'Hara?"

"O'Gara," I corrected with a snap.

"Can't say that I do. Did you know each other . . . back there?" He flapped his hand in the general direction of Yorkshire.

I didn't want to get Katie in trouble for doing anything "inappropriate." "We discovered we were distantly related."

"Ah, yes," he agreed. "You Americans are all so close."

What would I do if I never saw her again? Was I falling in love with her? A woman I barely knew? I smiled to myself, remembering my father telling me that all the Thomas men made spur-of-the-moment decisions. "Speed at grasping nettles," he had called it. And once, just once, DaDa let slip that he had proposed marriage to a woman he had just met. I had been avid to hear more, but he'd thought better of his revelation. He got that look the family called his "Black Welsh Face" and I didn't dare ask him any questions.

I looked at the tree, smoked another cigarette, and stared at the tapestry. Maybe she wasn't a shepherdess after all; the gown looked pretty grand. I wished there was a newspaper to read. I wished that Katie would come in. There  was a bustle, and Miss Rogers was back, with two more American nurses and an orderly. It was time for lunch, only Miss Rogers announced that it was "dinner." Christmas dinner.

"Roast lamb with mint sauce," Eli said approvingly. "Just what we used to have for Christmas back home. The only thing I miss is a glass of sherry. We always had sherry."

"We had sherry at our first meal together, Maggie. Do you remember?" DaDa poured a glass for her, and one for himself. It was a

holiday tradition, reserved for Thanksgiving, Christmas, and sometimes Easter, but only if Easter Sunday was a chilly day. With such rare use, the sherry decanter with its silver neck hanger never seemed depleted.

"No, Owen dear, we did not have sherry, because it was a Sunday and against the law. But I remember everything about that dinner. I remember thinking how handsome you were."

Tom and I waggled our eyebrows at each other, but for once, our mother missed the exchange. She was looking at my father. He patted her hand. "What I have always liked best about you, Maggie, is your honesty."

"I thought you loved me for my beauty," she teased.

"Oh, there was that, of course. Especially your nose." Tom and I waggled at each other again, but neither of our parents noticed.

"We always had sherry at Christmas, too." I came back to the present. "The year I turned eighteen, my parents asked me to join them for a glass. It was . . ." I groped for a superlative.

"The cat's meow," Ed Shank offered, and we all laughed. More nurses and orderlies came in and out with trays of food and pots of tea; several of them smiled at us, happy to hear us having a good time. I called out to the nearest one.

"Nurse. Nurse!" I hadn't seen this one before. She came

toward my bed. "There was a Miss O'Gara here last night, and I wondered what time she'd be back on duty. Do you know her?"

"Everybody knows Katie O'Gara." She was American. "Everybody *loves* Katie O'Gara." She said that with admiration, not a touch of malice. "She should be coming on night duty at eight. The parade of admirers starts at the door here. Join the crowd. Officers in front, other ranks behind." My expression must have given me away. She said quickly, with concern, "Are you in pain?"

"No. No," I said. "I guess I just need a cigarette."

The afternoon wore on. There wasn't much light to fade, but what there was of it went quickly. It's a sad time of day, these winter hours when darkness comes so early. The door to the ward kept opening and closing, but I didn't bother to look up any longer. So I didn't even see her come in.

"Was it a good Celtic Christmas, Mr. Thomas?"

I just stared at her. "You're early."

"Yes, I *am* early. Almost three hours early, as a matter of fact. But I couldn't wait another minute before—" She bit off the end of her sentence.

I hoped she had been about to say "before seeing you again." I hoped it so hard I almost heard her say it, but she didn't. I just lay there and looked up at her.

Katie was blushing, and hurried to change the subject. "What have you been doing here in the ward all day?"

"Thinking about you. Waiting for you to come. Thanking God that I was lucky enough to get a leave, and be in Piccadilly when the Zeppelin dropped the bomb. Otherwise we might never have met."

The blush deepened. She fumbled with her cloak. "Since I'm here, I'd better get to work."

"But you're not on duty until eight," I objected.

"I'm sure some of the nurses who have been here all day will be grateful to be relieved." I hadn't known Katie very long, but already I knew her well enough not to argue with her. "And after I finish my rounds, I'll bring you a nice cup of tea. Lie back, now. Try to go to sleep." I watched her move from bed to bed, taking temperatures, dispensing pills, holding water glasses, plumping pillows. For someone so young, she was quite a comforting woman. A comfortable woman.

I thought of the civilians who had been killed, of the men dying in the trenches of France. The world seemed very dark. A dark time to fall in love. Then I remembered my mother saying: "When you believe, the way is full of light. As happy as a Christmas tree with an angel at the top."

Suddenly, the lights of the Christmas tree blinked on. It

was a good Christmas after all. And that *was* a lovely tree, even though it didn't have an angel. In the dim light, I could almost imagine our angel at the top, just like always. Only, as I fell asleep, I thought: Funny, but she isn't wearing her crown this Christmas. She's wearing a white cap.

PART IV

Christmas in Bethlehem, 1934

James and Katie were married in 1920. They had two children: Nathaniel, known as Nat, and Katherine, my mother. This is the story of Nat and his Christmas tree, as my mother remembers it.

The coal regions of Pennsylvania had never been overly prosperous, and the Great Depression hit them hard. People seemed to age faster: boys became men overnight, and men became old men in one day when they saw their children hungry.

Nathaniel Thomas, Owen's grandson, was quite grown-up at ten.

Nat grew up on Owen's small farm on the outskirts of Bethlehem, with his grandfather; his parents, James and Katie; and his baby sister, Katherine. His grandmother, Maggie, died of pneumonia before he was born.

The farm was miles from town, and miles from the school-house; Nat had few friends his own age. His sister, only four, was too young to be a playmate. So he made a companion of the big blue spruce his grandfather planted the day he was born. He knew it was childish to make a secret playmate of the tree, but he was not quite ready to give up this comfort. The tree was his confidante, his advisor, his confessor, his best friend. When the wind stirred its branches, it made a humming sound. If Nat was lonely, he spoke to the tree and it always answered.

The last rays of the sun made the needles glint. Nat pulled his cap down lower over his ears and sniffed the November air. "It smells like snow," he told the tree. "I love snow, don't you?"

The tree's branches quivered in agreement. *Hmmm.*

"And after snow comes Christmas, and you'll have all your decorations, with the angel at the top." He stroked a branch, so prickly one way, so smooth the other. "You and

I are exactly the same age, do you know that? So how come you're so much taller?"

"Because blue spruce trees grow faster than boys. Simple as that."

"Grampa!" Owen Thomas was seventy-nine; life had weathered him, but not bent him an inch.

"Grampa, we were just talking about Christmas. And her decorations."

An icy rain began to fall. "We'd best go inside," Owen urged. But he could see the boy was reluctant to let go of this special moment, just the two of them and the tree. "Let's check on the Christmas ornaments. Might need some polishing." He tipped his cap to the tree. "We have to do this lady proud."

"Did you decorate a tree before I was born, Grampa? Before you planted my tree?"

"There was a blue spruce beside the house when we first came here, but it was struck by lightning the year before you were born. You were a good excuse for planting another one. But I gave this tree a field to herself, away from the house, where she'd have room to breathe."

They walked along the edge of the cornfield, past the pigpen, past the henhouse where Nat fed the chickens every morning and gathered the eggs after school every afternoon, past the tool shed. They stopped in at the barn and fed the two ever-hungry, contented cats who lived there. Owen put his arm around Nat's shoulder. "You're getting tall. But we are still going to need a ladder to put the angel on the top."

In the house, they opened the chest where the Christmas regalia was kept. The lazy Susan festooned with holly wreaths; a

cookie jar shaped like Santa Claus; big shiny balls of red and green and gold, heavier than most ornaments, meant for a tree that stands out of doors; swags of material that could stretch from branch to branch; soldiers, animals, birds, and cherubs cut from tin; sturdy containers that would hold birdseed.

And last of all, wrapped in a blue woolen shawl, was the angel. For Nat, the annual unwrapping of the angel was second only to the moment of placing her on top of the tree. He and his grandfather had a little ritual that went with the unwrapping. "And you carved her yourself?" Nat would always ask solemnly. And Owen would always reply, with equal solemnity: "Yes, I carved her myself, in Wales, many years ago when the world was young."

Nat held the angel carefully, touching the blue cloak, looking into the lavender eyes that always seemed mysterious. He began the litany. "And you carved her yourself?"

"Yes," Owen answered, and paused. "I carved her as a Christmas gift for the most beautiful woman in the world."

Nat gaped at him and pondered this new information. "For Grandma," he said with assurance. He had never known his grandmother, but he had seen photographs. She didn't look *that* beautiful, but even at ten he understood that you had to make allowances for love. Owen didn't reply; he was lost in thought. "For Grandma," Nat prompted again.

"No. Not for your grandmother. She was the *best* woman in the world, but she would be the first to admit not the most beautiful. No, Nat, I carved her for a remarkable woman named Jessica Lavery."

"Who was she, Grampa? Where is she now?"

Owen's eyes were distant. "She was an actress. A remarkable actress with lavender eyes. I believe she married an Englishman, and I believe they had children. I read that she died." There was a long silence and Nat knew that Owen was no longer speaking to him. "I have loved only two women in my life. And I have lost them both."

Nat longed to ask more questions, but Owen had that black look of his. The boy watched in silence as his grandfather dragged himself back to the present. He wrapped the angel back in the old blue shawl, then put his hand gently on Nat's head. "We'll be decorating the tree in another week." He was silent again, remembering. "Jessica agreed with me that a Christmas tree should always be outside, where—"

"Where it can look straight up to God," Nat completed the familiar story. He could hardly wait until tomorrow, when he could share this strange new turn of events with the tree.

The next day, a Sunday, was cold and dark; the sun was only a white ball low in the sky. As always, the Thomas family loaded into the Chevrolet to head to church. James drove, with Owen beside him; Nat and his mother sat in back, with Katherine between them, her feet just reaching the edge of the seat.

"Snow's in the air," James commented. "It's going to be a cold winter. You can tell because the squirrels all have thick coats and bushy tails."

"I think that's an old wives' tale about the squirrels." Katie was still quick at contraries. "But the Farmer's Almanac does predict it's going to be one of the snowiest winters in years. I just hope the storm holds off until we're home from church." Katie, maternal, worried, patted Katherine's hand.

"Maybe there won't be a storm," James teased his anxious wife.

"Oh, there's going to be a storm, all right. I can tell, because your limp is always a little heavier when bad weather's coming."

"We can turn back right now," James teased again.

"James Thomas, bite your tongue. Besides, the choir is singing a new hymn today, and we practiced it *twice* this week."

"What's the hymn, Katie?" Owen asked. "Sing us a verse or two?"

"I'll be happy to, it's such a lovely hymn. The words were just written, but they say the music is old." She sang:

> *Morning has broken, like the first morning,*
> *Blackbird has spoken, like the first bird.*
> *Praise for the singing,*
> *Praise for the morning,*
> *Praise for them springing fresh from the word.*

"Old music, is it?" Owen smiled. "Old as the hills, old as the druids. We used to sing the same tune with different words."

> *Child in the manger, infant of Mary,*
> *Outcast and stranger, Lord of all.*

Child who inherits
All our transgressions
All our demerits on Him fall.

"Sing it together?" Nat cajoled. Owen and Katie often sang duets—parlor songs, Katie called them—at home in the evening. They needed no coaxing. As they drove up to the church, they concluded in a burst of harmony.

Inside, the children trooped down to the basement for Sunday school. Katherine went to one room where the small children sat on tiny chairs at low tables and colored scenes from the Bible with fat crayons; Nat went to another where the older children opened folding chairs with a great clatter and recited, in unison, the psalm they had been required to memorize. This week it was "I will lift up mine eyes unto the hills." Maybe there were pretty hills in the Holy Land, Nat thought, but right here around *this* Bethlehem the hills are mostly slag heaps.

The children went upstairs to join their parents in church for the second part of the regular service. Nat noticed the platters with cubes of bread and the special round metal dishes with little goblets of grape juice. Today was a Communion Sunday. The ushers solemnly passed the plates from pew to pew and the minister spoke briefly. "We all have much to be thankful for, even in these difficult times. Let us thank God for our families, our friends, our loved ones—those with us now and those we have lost but will join again in Heaven." The choir stood to sing "Morning Has Broken," and Nat could pick out his mother's determined soprano, slightly off pitch on the high notes.

Sunday dinner was special, even in the midst of winter, even in the midst of a Depression. Nat's Sunday chore, which he enjoyed, was to set the table with the good china that was usually on display in the oak breakfront. They ate in the kitchen, warmed by the fire in the big black coal stove that was never allowed to go out, and cheered by the oilcloth table cover with its strawberry clusters.

Katie brought a casserole to the table, and they all bowed their heads as Owen said grace. "I thought about stewing a chicken," Katie announced, as she ladled. "But then I thought of how much happier we would all be if we *sold* the chicken instead of *eating* it. So I made a vegetable stew instead. All good things from the root cellar— potatoes, onions, turnips, corn, lima beans, parsnips . . ."

"I don't like parsnips," little Katherine objected.

"I like parsnips a lot," Nat lied politely.

"I like parsnips a lot too," Katherine echoed. "I like everything Nat likes. But the ones I like best are the green ones that say they love you."

"What in the world are they?" James asked.

"She means lima beans," Nat explained. "They're sort of shaped like hearts."

"Nat always knows what I mean." Katherine was solemn.

"I listen hard to you," Nat said. "I always do."

"This is excellent, Katie," Owen offered. "Chicken stew without the chicken reminds me of the recipe for Welsh soup. You know how to make Welsh soup?" The family all shook their heads. "You fill a pot with water, add one big stone, and set it on a fire beside the roadside. Along comes someone who says: 'Hello! Why are you cooking a stone there?' And you explain that you are making soup. So the person takes pity on you for being a poor, dumb Welshman, and adds some potatoes. And the next person comes along and says: 'That's not a proper soup. Just a stone and some poor old potatoes,' and contributes some beans. And so it goes until finally somebody pitches in a chicken. Then you remove the stone and serve the meal. And that, my darlings, is how you make Welsh soup."

Everyone applauded. "Thanks, Dad," James said. "It's been a tough year, but we're making it, aren't we? It could be worse." Then, with a grin, to Katie, "Remember Eli Scruggs and his 'Amen Stew'?"

"I remember every single thing about the hospital and Eli Scruggs and Ed Shank. And you." Katie could still blush. She and James smiled at each other in silence, while the children stared.

Owen rescued them. "We'll be able to have chicken for Christmas Day. You know, I'm almost glad we can't afford goose. I never told your mother, James, but I really didn't like it. I miss the lamb, though. Pennsylvania lamb is good, even if it isn't as good as Welsh mutton, which is—"

"The best in the world," James, Katie, and Nat chorused, and they laughed together.

"One of these days, we'll be able to afford lamb for Christmas again, you'll see," Owen predicted.

"And Christmas cookies," James added. "Remember Mama's Christmas cookies—enough to last until Easter?"

"She taught me how to make snickerdoodles," Katie remembered. "Oh, and one day we'll have champagne again."

"Yes." Owen smiled at his daughter-in-law. "To delight your Southern soul. Yes, we have a lot to be thankful for. We don't have dust storms in Pennsylvania. And we have a president who cares about farmers."

"And a first lady who cares about them too," Katie added.

"I like Mrs. Roosevelt," Nat said.

"I like Mrs. Roosevelt, too," Katherine echoed.

After dinner, Nat went to visit his tree and discuss Owen's startling disclosure. "So there are two women Grampa has loved in his lifetime. *Two!* But I guess I think that's okay, don't you?" The tree shook its boughs gently in agreement. *Hmmm.*

When Owen appeared, as Nat knew he would, they walked together toward the house, the corn stubble and the snow crunching under their boots. "Grampa, the minister said this morning that we would join our loved ones in Heaven." Owen nodded. "Are you going to join Grandma *and* the beautiful actress at the same time?"

Owen laughed his great young laugh. "Nat, that is a question I have asked myself a thousand times. And at last I have the answer." Nat waited. "I am leaving that to God. Now let's go inside and finish polishing the ornaments. Just a few more days and we'll be decorating the tree."

But the little town of Bethlehem, Pennsylvania, had other ideas.

For years, during the Christmas holidays, the township had set up a manger scene in the center square. Each year, it had become more elaborate, adding shepherds here and angels there, a more elegant crown for one of the magi, a calf or two to the sleepy cows. Spotlights soon made the crèche come alive at night. Gradually, local schools and churches began to vie for the privilege of singing carols on the square, until there was almost constant musical entertainment.

As the Depression took hold, the town fathers began to notice that Bethlehem was becoming a tourist attraction for the surrounding area. It didn't cost much to drive into town to see the manger and listen to the carolers. It cost only three cents to buy a stamp and mail a letter postmarked "Bethlehem."

In November, the wife of one of Bethlehem's burgesses had a wonderful idea. She had been reading about the celebrated Christmas tree in Rockefeller Center, about to be installed for the second year, and already a tradition. Well, she reasoned to her husband, why shouldn't Bethlehem have a tree that is just as famous? Not as big, of course, because it must be in proportion with the crèche. But a tree as beautiful, no, *more beautiful* than the one in New York. So they would have a contest to choose the most beautiful tree in all the surrounding countryside. And—here was her biggest idea— offer a prize of twenty-five dollars!

Searchers fanned out all over the county; they photographed and sketched and measured and argued. And finally, on the second day of December, a winner was chosen. James Thomas came to tell his father and his son that the Tree of Bethlehem was to be Nat's blue spruce. If Nat and Owen would agree.

"You planted it, DaDa," James said. "And you have cherished it, son. I know twenty-five dollars is not a great deal of money, but we could buy your mother something for Christmas, Nat, that would make her eyes dance. And some clothing for your little sister, who is wearing hand-me-downs and smells like a cedar trunk. No, twenty-five dollars is not life-or-death for this family at this moment, praise God, but it will keep the house warm and keep food on the table until spring comes."

Owen did not speak. He simply fixed his eyes on his grandson. Nat spoke very fast, the way people do when they are trying to get the words out without crying. He said of course they must sell the tree and buy a present for his mother and clothes for his sister and coal for the furnace and food for the table. There could always be another tree, he said.

Then he hurried outside and ran to the tree, put his hands as far around the trunk as he could reach, and buried his head in its branches. That was where Owen found him.

Nat stayed home from school the next day when they came to cut down the tree. He didn't want to be there, but he couldn't be away. Both his parents, normally strict about attendance, pretended he wasn't well. "You're looking a little peaked," his mother clucked. She put a cool nurse's hand on his forehead. "Best stay at home today."

So Nat was in the yard when the truck pulled up, and the two men in overalls peered out. "Thomas Farm?" one asked. "Christmas tree farm?" Nat, silent, nodded and pointed and led the way to the tree.

"Hey, that's a swell tree. A swell tree!" the taller one said.

"What d'ya call this kind of tree?" the shorter one asked. He took out the chain saw.

"It's a blue spruce," Nat replied, and ran across the fields to the far side of the farm. He put his hands over his ears so he wouldn't hear the whine of the saw. Even so, he thought he heard the tree crying out to him.

The next day, when Nat came home from school, his

grandfather and Katherine were inspecting the Christmas ornaments. "I thought we might decorate the spruce near the barn," Owen invited. "Not a bad little tree. Not a beauty, but it shows promise."

Nat shook his head angrily. How could any other tree deserve this honor? How dare any other tree wear the regalia?

Owen held up the angel. "Does that mean she won't grace a tree this Christmas?"

"No!" Nat growled and reached for the angel blindly, accidentally knocking her out of his grandfather's hands. She fell to the kitchen floor. Nat and Owen were frozen, so it was Katherine who picked the angel up and turned her face toward them.

"She breaked her nose," Katherine announced sadly. The wood had crumbled away.

"Her nose is smashed! I smashed her nose. Oh, Grampa, I'm sorry. Oh, angel, I'm sorry." Nat turned to his grandfather. "But you can fix her." It was a statement, not a question.

"Nat, there are some things you can't ever fix, no matter how much you want to, no matter how sorry you are. I'm afraid this is one of them." He put his arm around Nat's shoulders. "She may not be quite as beautiful, but don't you think her nose has given her a lot of character?"

It snowed the morning of Christmas Eve. Not enough to cover over the slag heaps that rimmed the town, but enough to gentle them. In the town square, volunteers were putting finishing touches on the crèche. Although it had been in place for weeks, now was the time for last-minute touches. Men were screwing more colored lights into sockets, testing connections, muttering in exasperation as some lights blinked on and others blinked off. Women were arranging fresh pine boughs for artistic effect; some here to mask a place where the paint had peeled from the crib; some there to make a canopy for the figure of Mary or a place for the oxen to lie. A small group of experts prepared the explosives for the midnight fireworks.

At the Thomas farm, Owen and Nat watched the snow fall. "In Wales, we would always hope for enough snow so we could hitch the horse to the sleigh to ride to chapel in grand style on Christmas Eve. But for tonight, we must hope there is not too much snow, not enough to interfere with the lighting of the manger."

He left unspoken "and the lighting of the Christmas tree," but he and Nat had what they called Welsh telepathy. "We do not need to tip tables or have séances or summon spirits from the vasty deep," Owen had said once. "Nat and I have the gift of the Old People, to speak to each other without speaking."

"At least she will be outside, where she can look straight up to God," Nat answered.

"Yes," Owen replied. No "Amen" could have been more profound. There was a silence between them of complete understanding.

It was broken by honking, of both car horn and geese. James and Katie Thomas were home from Christmas errands, with little Katherine in tow. Katie filled the kitchen with activity; put a flame under the teakettle, opened the potato sack, took down the flour, mopped a spill on the floor with an old cloth and her left foot.

"Nathaniel, you must get on your dancing slippers for tonight, for I'll be having the third dance with you. Your father the first, your grampa the second, and my tall, handsome son I'll be proud to have as my third partner." Katie took her son's hands, pantomimed a dance. "And they say there will be fiddlers from three counties, and that the governor's wife is coming herself to see the best crèche and the most beautiful Christmas tree in the state . . ."

She stopped in mid-sentence, aware this was a painful topic for her son. Nat looked at her gratefully; his mother understood what the tree meant to him.

It was already dark at six o'clock as they drove into Bethlehem and parked near the center square. Nat held the angel, wrapped in the old blue shawl; he and his grandfather had agreed they would let her grace the city's tree for this one night only, as a farewell.

The tree was not there. A busy policeman explained that the town fathers had decided to hold the Christmas tree lighting in the rotunda of City Hall because of the snowy weather.

And there, indeed, she was, on a stand that loudly played carols as it revolved. The tree was covered with blinking lights and frosted glass balls. Nat worked his way through the crowd to get closer. "You're *inside*," he whispered. "You've never been inside before. You don't like it, do you?"

The tree did not answer. It seemed to Nat that the stand was spinning her against her will, and although she revolved, her branches did not move. "Talk to me," he begged, but the tree said nothing. "Please," he whispered. The lights blinked on and off and the music played, but the tree was silent, silent as death. Nat stood there for several minutes, then hugged the angel to his chest and hurried out of the building.

✳

In the months that followed, Nat avoided walking anywhere near the field where the tree had stood. Spring and summer came and went; nobody in the household mentioned the blue spruce, and they even banned the word "tree" from conversation. There was a dusting of snow early in November, and Katie held a conference with Owen about the coming holiday. He suggested they wait a while longer. "Sometimes time heals," he said. "Sometimes miracles happen."

One late November afternoon, Nat put his schoolbooks in his room and came back outside. Snow was in the air; another Christmas was coming. He decided not to think about it.

"Nat." He turned to see his sister. "I have a s'prise to show you."

"A surprise?"

"C'mon." She tugged at his hand, and they set out across the field. Katherine was wheeling a small, rather battered doll carriage. It bumped over the corn stubble. "Do you really have to take the carriage?" he asked her.

"Yes," she said. "I need it."

He realized that she was taking him to the spot where his tree had stood. "Where are we . . . why are we . . . ?" He stopped to look at his sister.

"Are you coming?"

"Of course I am." They continued walking.

Katherine pointed. "Look."

There, in the very center of the stump, a tiny blue spruce was growing. He came toward it, holding his breath.

"Tree?"

And in a sweet young voice, it hummed to him.

He turned to Katherine, but she was bending over the doll carriage. When she straightened up, he saw that in her arms she held the Christmas angel. "How did you know about the tree?" he asked her.

"I watered it in the summer." Katherine held the angel up beside the tree. "But the angel is too big. The tree is too little."

"Blue spruce trees grow very fast," Nat reassured her. "Grampa said so. In just a year or two, the tree will be tall enough to support the angel on top. In the meantime, she can guard us all from below. We'll make a special manger scene for her."

"Hold your angel, Nat."

"No, let her stay in your arms, Katherine," he said. "She is your angel, too. Oh, she is very much your angel, too."

PART V

Christmas in New York, 1959

This is the story of Nat's little sister: my mother, Katherine Thomas. How she became Kitsey. And then became Katherine again.

Kitsey looked up at the tree that towered over Rockefeller Plaza. You may think you are the best tree in the world, she told it silently, but you aren't. I know one that is not as tall, but far more beautiful.

Some evenings, on the way from her office to the subway, Kitsey stopped to watch the skaters, but tonight she was in a hurry to get home. She was carrying an important pre-Christmas gift. Well, when you consider I'm also carrying the baby, I guess it's *two* gifts, she thought. It was the first time in the seven months of her pregnancy that she thought of the baby as a gift, rather than a bit of a nuisance.

"Katherine! Katherine Thomas!" The woman stopped Kitsey, put a hand on her shoulder. "Don't you remember me? I must have been calling you for half a block!"

"Oh, Mrs. Pasek, I'm so sorry." It was the mother of one of her high school classmates from Bethlehem. "But everybody calls me Kitsey now, so I don't think of myself as Katherine. How is Dolores? Where is she? What are you doing in New York?"

"Dolores is still living at home with us, but she's about to announce her engagement. A very nice young man from Pittsburgh. Not Polish, but a very nice young man. Her father and I are very pleased." Mrs. Pasek blew her nose. "Goodness, it's windy on this corner. I'm just in New York for the day. Came on a chartered bus with the Saint Anne's ladies to see the Christmas Show at Radio City." She blew her nose again.

"And no need to ask what's new with *you*, I guess. When are you due?"

"The middle of February. Please tell Dolores congratulations and send my love."

"And congratulations to you, Kath . . . what did you say your name is now?"

"Kitsey. Kitsey Gottlieb." She watched Mrs. Pasek disappear into the crowd. But I'm also still Katherine Thomas, she reminded herself. There are lots of parts to me.

✳

She had been transformed into Kitsey just before Christmas of her freshman year at Thornton College.

Her sorority big sister gave her the name. "Katherine seems awfully . . . I don't know . . . austere for a bouncy person like you. You seem more like a Kitsey to me." The sisters who were lounging around the Beta suite in Hunt Hall agreed. Many of them in this sorority had nicknames like Binky and Dodie and Muffy; "Kitsey" fit right in.

Beta Omega was the sorority for campus leaders. Tri Delts were the best-looking; Pi Phis were the athletes; but the Betas ran the school. So Kitsey (still Katherine at the time) had been thrilled that the Betas seemed to want her. On the first night of Freshman Rush Week, she had accepted the invitation to their reception. She looked around at the editor of the newspaper, the president of the drama club, the head of the Women's Student Government Association, and thought: Oh, yes, please, this is where I want to be.

On the second night of Rush she visited the Pi Phis, and on the third night—just to assure herself that she wasn't being a snob—went to the Zeta reception. It was the only sorority that accepted Jews, blacks, intellectuals, and eccentrics. Katherine sipped her tea and noticed that this was the smallest and most subdued group of the three. She tried unsuccessfully to feel at home.

Saturday night was the culmination of Rush Week, the night when the sororities officially welcomed their new pledges. The invitations were slipped under the doors of the chosen before seven o'clock that morning. Katherine and her roommate Molly watched as three envelopes slid into the room. "I don't think I can stand this one more minute." Molly tore open the one envelope with her name, opened the letter, shrieked, and waved it in the air. "Tri Delt! The only one I wanted!"

The other two envelopes revealed that both the Betas and the Zetas were asking Katherine Thomas to join their sisterhood. Katherine thought about how good it would make her feel to accept the Zetas' offer, about the jubilation in their suite as they opened the RSVPs and saw her name, about the nobility of her sacrifice, casting her lot with the disenfranchised. She picked up a pen and firmly circled the "Regrets" on one invitation and "Accepts" on the other.

"So?" Molly asked. "What did you decide?"

"Beta," Katherine said.

She arrived that evening at the sorority suite in the skirt and white blouse they had all been asked to wear for the ceremony. There was solemn singing, solemn vows were exchanged, and each new pledge received a white rose as a symbol of purity. At the end of the hour, as Katherine and the other freshmen went down the big circular staircase in Hunt Hall, the Betas hung over the balustrade and sang a farewell song.

And so Katherine became a Beta. And then she became Kitsey.

✳

Two months later, she sat in the chilly Edwards Lakes to Sea bus, heading home to Bethlehem for Christmas. My feet are cold. My fingers are cold. I can almost see my breath. For what they charge from Thornton to Bethlehem they should be able to heat the damn thing. The bus groaned its way through the little towns of the Coal Region. Mauch Chunk. Mahanoy

City. Pottsville. Shamokin. Ashland, where her grandparents had lived, she a teacher, he a miner, before they came to the farm.

Kitsey thought of the Christmases of her childhood, of how Nat and their grandfather were always in charge of the Christmas tree decorations. She was so proud when Nat decided she was old enough to handle the angel carefully, and gave her the honor of unwrapping it every year from the blue shawl that had belonged to her great-grandmother. And every year, on January 6, they would take down the ornaments and put them away. Kitsey smiled to herself as she remembered how her mother always took down the tinsel, strand by strand, laboriously smoothed it out, and put it away in the Christmas chest. Her father always teased her about that. "Nobody saves *tinsel*, for Pete's sake." And then, when the war came and silver foil was not available, they were the only family she knew who still had tinsel strips on their tree.

She was eleven when the war began, and Nat was seventeen. He constantly pestered James for permission to enlist, but James refused. "You have plenty of time," he told Nat over and over. "Plenty of time." Nat waited impatiently for the year to pass, and on the day he was eighteen, joined the navy. All he wanted, he told his parents, was for the war to last long enough for him to see action.

Then Nat's cruiser was sunk in the Pacific. "I guess he didn't have plenty of time after all," James said. Her mother cried when they unwrapped the ornaments that year, and said that the tree and the angel could look up to God if they wanted to, but she wasn't so sure God was bothering to look back down. So Katherine decorated the tree—she still thought of it as Nat's tree—with her father and grandfather. There was no teasing about tinsel. And Katherine mourned quietly for the brother who had listened hard to her and always knew what she meant.

The next year, her grandfather died. Her mother said: "Maybe this year, to honor Owen's memory, we shouldn't have a big Christmas or decorate the tree." Her father said: "This year, in his honor, we *must* decorate the tree." So Kitsey and her father took out the Christmas chest and she unwrapped the angel, and together they decorated Nat's tree. Her father didn't cry, but his voice was husky as he placed the angel on its top. "Now they can look straight up to God. And straight up to a couple of his newer angels."

✳

During her four years at Thornton, Kitsey outdid the Betas. She was head of the drama club, editor of the yearbook, and a Phi Beta Kappa. Her favorite professor, chairman of the

English Department, took her for coffee one morning just before graduation. They sat facing each other in the grimy old pre-fab building that was the faculty lounge. "Kitsey," he said, "you don't have to do *everything*, you know."

"But I want to. And I *can*."

Dr. Jones shook his head. "Something might get left behind."

"What would that be?"

"Time to think." He took a sip of his coffee. "Time to love."

"Oh, I'll make time for that," Kitsey laughed. "I'll make time when I have the time."

She thought that was a funny line, but Professor Jones looked sad. "Be careful, Kitsey," he said. "You may lose something."

✳

Kitsey was infatuated with New York. She worked for her first year as an assistant in the research department of a weekly newsmagazine. But it was really a secretarial job, and she didn't have steno. Her second year, through a Thornton contact, she landed a spot as a production assistant on a new soap opera. But it wasn't renewed. The third year, she read an article in *Cosmopolitan* about how to land a job in publishing. She wangled an interview at Suffolk Press, one of the hot new

publishing houses, hit it off with the editor who spoke with her, and was hired as a junior editor. She was in thrall.

The walk-up apartment she shared with two roommates was small, and the walls were thin. They complained to Kitsey that her typing kept them awake after midnight and woke them up on weekend mornings. They said she had so many manuscripts piled in the living room, their dates couldn't sit down. Kitsey simply worked harder than ever, and as soon as she received her first promotion and a raise, she moved into a studio apartment of her own. There, she was able to work all the time.

Her office mate at Suffolk, a fellow editor and recent bride, took as her avocation finding the perfect man for Kitsey.

"I've had it with blind dates," Kitsey said. "One disaster after another."

"He's really awfully nice," Gloria offered.

"I'd rather stay home with the manuscript of a bad first novel than go out on another boring first date."

"He's well educated," Gloria persisted. "He's good-looking."

"Um."

"He's an architect."

"That's kind of interesting. I read *The Fountainhead* at Thornton."

"He's a Yalie. From New Jersey, but lives in New York now. And he's Jewish."

"Sounds possible. Name?"

"David Gottlieb. I'll tell him to pick you up at your apartment at seven o'clock and we'll all have dinner together."

"What makes you so sure David Gottlieb will want to have a blind date with me?"

"Because I already asked him."

So Kitsey Thomas and David Gottlieb met for the first time in October 1957. David rang her doorbell a few minutes after seven. Gloria had been accurate for once, Kitsey conceded to herself; he *is* good-looking. By the time they had finished dinner in the trendy restaurant, she decided he was also well educated. By the time he escorted her back to her apartment door, she wasn't quite ready to see him go, and invited him in for coffee.

David asked her about the books she was working on, and listened with such interest that she told him all about the Mary Todd Lincoln biography. "The author never thinks her writing is good enough. I have to coax every chapter out of her."

David asked her about herself. "What kind of a name is Kitsey?"

"It's one of the nicknames for Katherine."

"Well, it ranks right up there with those other famous WASP nicknames like Binky. My grandfather the rabbi would be shocked to know I am dating a girl named Kitsey."

"A shiksa named Kitsey."

He raised his eyebrows in approval. "How do you know any Yiddish?"

"I dated a few Sammies at Thornton. They were Sigma Alpha Mu—the Jewish fraternity."

"I know."

"Did you belong to a fraternity?"

"Kitsey, studying architecture is almost like pre-med. No, it's more like preparing for the priesthood. You don't have time for anything else. You don't *want* time for anything else."

"But you had time for *me* tonight." She couldn't help flirting.

"Even architects have feast days, but they are rare. If we are going to see each other, you need to understand that. And you will, won't you, Kitsey?"

"Yes, David," she said.

A long two weeks elapsed before they saw each other again. David called her at the office. "How is the reluctant Lincoln biographer?"

"You remembered that." Kitsey wondered why this pleased her so much. "My brother used to call that 'listening hard.'"

"I don't 'listen hard' to everybody, Kitsey, but I do to you. And I'm sorry to call you at the last minute, but it's one of those rare architectural feast days. Will you have sushi with me tonight?"

Of course he knew the most authentic sushi restaurant in the city, tucked away on the second floor of a nondescript West Side building. "Lovely sushi," she said, and took a sip of warm sake from the tiny cup.

They had been talking about publishing, and David had listened attentively to her dreams of becoming a great editor, the kind of editor who would nurture young writers, discover another James Joyce. Now they turned to architecture. "What kind of courses do you take to study architecture?" she asked him.

"Lots of stuff you'll never need again in real life, because there are experts you hire, but you need the courses for the degree. Things like plumbing." Kitsey laughed. "Electrical engineering, heating and ventilating, surveying, mechanical engineering."

"No literature courses?" Kitsey had been an English major; literature was food and drink to her.

"Maybe one course that could even be considered liberal arts. An art and architecture survey—from Babylon to the Bauhaus in one semester."

"But no literature courses." Kitsey grieved for him.

"If we are going to see more of each other—and I hope we are—you will have to realize that I am visual, not verbal. I'm not going to sit beside you at the fireside reading Virginia Woolf; I'm not going to read poetry to you."

"I could read poetry to *you*."

There was a long silence. "I'm not sure I'd like it. Would you miss that part?"

Another memory nagged at her. It was a passage from one of her grandmother Maggie's journals. They were considered a family treasure, and Kitsey had read through them all avidly when she was in high school. What was she remembering? She turned her attention back to David Gottlieb. He will be a famous architect and I will be a famous editor. What more could we ask? "I think I'll get all the literature I need right at my job."

"Then we'll see, shall we, Kitsey?"

"Yes, David."

Their friends all marveled at the whirlwind courtship. Even Gloria asked Kitsey if she didn't think they were rushing things a bit. "It runs in the Thomas family," Kitsey told her serenely. "Speed at grasping nettles." They were married in February 1958 by a New York City judge, the friend of one of the senior partners in David's firm. They had briefly discussed a religious ceremony and just as briefly dismissed it. David didn't belong to a synagogue in New York and didn't know a rabbi. He thought his parents would be uncomfortable at a church service. "You sure you don't mind?" he asked. "We've never discussed religion in any depth. You're not really religious, are you?"

Kitsey caught herself remembering all those Sunday mornings at the Bethlehem Presbyterian Church; about putting her penny in the collection basket at Sunday school; about her mother and grandfather singing "Morning has broken, like the first morning" and "Holy, holy, holy, Lord God Almighty."

"No," she said with less than her usual certainty. "No, I'm not really religious. Not deeply anyway."

They telephoned both sets of parents, and went off for the weekend to a Victorian bed-and-breakfast in Connecticut. Both agreed they were too busy for a honeymoon: David was designing the national headquarters for a bank; Kitsey was working with two authors on big fall books. "We'll have a proper honeymoon this summer," David promised. "Two whole weeks. I'll show you the cathedrals of Britain."

"And Westminster Abbey," Kitsey added.

"Sure, but don't try to get me to Poets' Corner." They both smiled.

They rented a one-bedroom apartment on West Eighty-eighth Street, with a minuscule kitchenette behind a folding door, and a fire escape, where Kitsey immediately placed a potted geranium. "We're home," she declared. The Thomases were the first to visit. They had liked David from the first, for the seriousness of his professional bent and his obvious adoration of Kitsey. When Kitsey was in the kitchen, she overheard her mother whispering to her father about their apartment décor: "Austere, isn't it?"

Next the Gottliebs came to visit. They, too, were happy. They, too, had approved of the match from its very beginning, but Kitsey's dedication to her publishing career concerned them. "You are going to have children, aren't you?" Mrs. Gottlieb asked just before they left, hugging Kitsey good-bye.

"Oh, yes," Kitsey answered truthfully. "Oh, yes, but not just yet."

They managed to make their vacations coincide for ten days in August, and did indeed visit several English cathedrals. David was a knowing guide, full of curious anecdotes and little-known facts; pointing out where a central tower collapsed in 1350, why an angry sculptor carved a gargoyle to resemble the archbishop. When they stopped in Cambridge, he took her punting on the Cam. "See that big willow beside the bridge? When a Cambridge man proposes to his girl, he usually does so beneath that willow."

Kitsey asked him how he knew so much about the local customs.

"I spent my junior year here at Cambridge," he told her.

"Oh," she said.

"Kitsey, I guess there's a lot we still don't know about each other."

Back in New York, they settled into a hardworking routine. They usually stayed at their offices until seven or eight every night, and worked all day most Saturdays. "Let's promise to keep Sundays for ourselves," David urged. She agreed, but sometimes, when he was reading the Sunday paper, she sneaked in some editing.

In December 1958, just before their first Christmas, David announced that he was going to buy some holiday decorations. Kitsey was delighted. "I didn't expect you to put up a tree!"

"I wasn't thinking of a tree." Her face must have fallen. "You don't really want a tree, do you? In this little apartment? And isn't a Christmas tree really a little ta—" Kitsey knew he was going to say "tacky" but he caught himself. "A little too much?"

This would be the first Christmas of her life without a tree. "No, darling, I don't really need one. *You* light up my life."

David gave a mock groan. "Once a writer, always a writer." He bought three silver globes at Georg Jensen's and hung them in the archway between the bedroom and the hall. Kitsey told him they were lovely, but she couldn't help remembering her mother's whisper: "Austere."

"I'm going to bake Christmas cookies," Kitsey announced. "The way my mother always did; the way my grandmother taught her. Snickerdoodles and oatmeal drop cookies. And I'll buy some cookie cutters so I can bake bells and tin soldiers and things."

Christmas Eve, on their way to the supermarket, they

passed a sidewalk stand selling trees. "Don't they smell wonderful!" Kitsey sighed, breathing in. "Look at all the needles they're dropping already," David countered. But he bought a holly wreath for their front door. "Peace offering," he said.

Kitsey hugged him. "What do you want to do tomorrow?" she asked. "Shall we go out for Christmas dinner? Or would you rather stay at home? We always had a leg of lamb for Christmas, lamb and cham-pagne. It seems silly to do a big roast just for the two of us, but we *could* have champagne. What did your family do for Christmas?"

"What do Jewish families always do for Christmas? There's a standard answer to that question. Eat at a Chinese restaurant and go to the movies. My father didn't like Chinese food, so we always had pizza on Christmas Day instead. Then we went to a movie."

David and Kitsey settled on pizza and champagne for their Christmas dinner. "We're establishing a new tradition," he laughed.

The Gottliebs came from New Jersey to visit on New Year's Day. Over dinner, at the tiny table that doubled as David's drawing desk, Kitsey talked about their vacation plans. "We had such a good time doing English cathedrals, we thought this summer we'd do Romanesque churches in Normandy."

"Wouldn't you rather have a baby than some old Romanesque churches?" Mrs. Gottlieb asked.

Kitsey was quick with an answer. "We definitely want to have children. But not yet. My publishing house just gave me the next book from one of our most important authors, so I'm going to be awfully busy." She apologized for the bakery store cookies she was passing with the coffee. "I meant to bake Christmas cookies, but somehow I ran out of time."

Kitsey was astounded, and a bit resentful, when in June she learned that she was pregnant.

With a child, possibly a son, on the way, David suddenly became what he laughingly termed "much more of a Jew." They discussed names for the baby, of course. David suggested

Samuel for a boy, after his great-grandfather. "But they'll call him Sammy," Kitsey protested. "Not if we insist his name is Samuel," David said. And that was that.

For a girl's name they settled on Susan. They discovered that each of them had an aunt named Susan. Well, David's aunt was actually Shoshanna, but he said it was close enough.

David began to go to Saturday morning services at a synagogue near their apartment. Kitsey offered to go with him, but David said he didn't know himself whether he would keep on attending; why didn't they just wait and see. But he did keep on.

By late November of 1959, Kitsey was almost seven months pregnant, feeling physically fit and almost daring the pregnancy to slow her down. The other women in her Lamaze childbirth class teased her about being the only one of them still able to run for the crosstown bus. "What am I supposed to do?" she asked David. "Sit home and watch my stomach?"

She was still working nine- and ten-hour days, bringing home editing projects at night and on weekends. As soon as dinner was over, Kitsey routinely climbed into bed with a manuscript in her hands and worked for a few more hours. One evening David came in and sat down on the bed beside her. "Will you put the papers down for a minute, please."

His tone got her attention. "Is something wrong?"

"I'm not sure," David answered. "We never have time to talk anymore."

"Oh, darling, we can fix that. Just let me finish editing this chapter and I'll come right out so we can chat."

An hour later, Kitsey came out of the bedroom. David looked up from his drawing board. "So, darling, what did you want to talk about?" she asked brightly.

"Nothing really, I guess."

"You don't seem to listen hard to me lately." Kitsey pouted slightly.

"Maybe it's because, lately, you haven't been saying very much to me. We're losing something, Kitsey. I miss you."

That December, New York City had a record snowfall, Christmas and Hanukkah almost coincided, and Kitsey and David had the first serious argument of their marriage—about where to spend the holiday.

"Look what my mother sent me!" Before David could take his coat off, Kitsey held out the angel. "My grandfather carved her in Wales. Isn't she beautiful? She was always at the top of our tree every Christmas since I can remember. Mom wants us to have her now, for our own tree, because of the baby. To carry on the tradition."

David examined the angel gently. "A Victorian beauty. What happened to her nose?"

"My brother dropped her one Christmas. My grandfather said it reminded him of my grandmother's snub nose; it added to her character."

"We could hang her right here in the archway, instead of the globes."

"She has to be on a *tree*! And the tree has to be outdoors where she can look straight up to God." All at once there were tears in her eyes. "Oh, David, the angel makes me so homesick. I didn't realize how much I wanted to be home in Bethlehem for Christmas."

He looked as stern as an Old Testament prophet. "I was hoping we could visit my folks during Hanukkah; I've let them down for years."

"Please! We can celebrate Christmas *and* Hanukkah at my home."

"I suspect there aren't many menorahs for sale in Bethlehem, Pennsylvania." David put on his coat. "And, by the way, Mrs. Gottlieb, I rather thought that *this* was your home."

"Where are you going?"

"Back to the office. I need to get a lot of design work done before we leave for Bethlehem."

His tone was icy. Kitsey thought he might just as well have said: "Before we leave for Hell." She waited for the door to slam, but it didn't, and his self-control upset her even further. The baby kicked hard enough to make her sit down. She picked up the angel for comfort, felt its warmth against her palms. "What do you think I should do?" she asked. "If Granmpa were here, what would he say? What would Nat say? I love David very much, you know. So much that, if he asked me, I would wrap you back in the Welsh shawl and put you away for a thousand years."

Kitsey sat there for a long time, one hand holding the angel, one hand on her stomach, feeling the baby swimming strongly. She had planned to use this time to read a new manuscript, but now she had something more important to accomplish.

The next evening, David was in the apartment when Kitsey came in from work. "You're home early!" she greeted him.

"Last-minute shopping," he said, and nodded at the shopping bag she carried. "I see you were doing some yourself."

"Yes. A surprise. A surprise for you. I thought I would beat you home today and have it all ready for you, so now you are going to have to turn around and close your eyes until I tell you it's ready." David obeyed, making mock noises of protest. Kitsey worked quickly. "Okay."

On the table was a menorah, with the candles ready to be

lighted. "I know we light the shammes candle first, and use that candle to light the others. And I know we say a prayer: 'God bless the lighting of this candle . . .' "

"Kitsey." David was stunned.

"And that's another thing. I'm going to be Katherine from now on. Katherine again. 'Whither thou goest, I will go . . .' "

He held out his arms and she went into them. "I have found the one whom my soul loves," he whispered to her.

"The Song of Solomon," she marveled. "And the King James Version at that!"

"I'm not totally illiterate, you know." David took her hand. "Now it's time for your surprise. I'm glad we are making some new traditions, but you shouldn't have to give up the old ones. They're too important." He led her to the window that opened onto the fire escape. There stood a Christmas tree with the angel at the top. Now it was Katherine's turn to be stunned. Silent, she simply reached out and touched the branches with her fingertips.

David was solemn. "Last night after you fell asleep, I picked up the angel and she told me what I should do."

"I know. Yesterday she did the same thing for me. David, the tree is perfect."

"Well, not exactly perfect. The angel can't look quite straight up to God, because the fire escape above us blocks the view. Can a Christmas tree crane its neck?"

"*Our* Christmas tree can do anything!"

"And anyway," David said, "I don't think God lets a fire escape or two get in His way." He took her hand. "Do you still want to go home to Bethlehem for Christmas? We will, my darling, if you like."

"I *am* home."

"Yes."

They stood there at the open window, hand in hand, mindless of the cold, looking at the tree. And the baby leaped. And the angel smiled.

PART VI

Christmas in Wales, 1990

I t's time for me to introduce myself. I'm Susan Gottlieb, daughter of David and Katherine, and the family historian. I have wondered what drove me to write this chronicle; what made me need to explore the secret compartments in women's desks and men's hearts. My family history has always been a puzzle to me. I thought that if I could put the pieces together, I would uncover the message, solve the mystery. So let me begin at the beginning, where I enter the story.

"You're going to do *what?*" everybody asked me in disbelief. At the age of thirty, I announced that I was quitting my job at a magazine in New York and moving to London to set up my own business as a photographer's representative. I had to explain that repping a photographer is like being a literary agent, except instead of sending manuscripts to publishers, you show sample photos to people who might like to buy them, or hire the photographer to do a new shoot. But most people were still thunderstruck by my decision. "Giving up your career!" they protested. "Leaving New York!"

London would be my first foray into the Susan Gottlieb Photography Representation business. My own company. A little scary, because I'd always had a safety net under me. First my parents; then a publishing house (introduced by Mom); then an architectural firm (courtesy of Dad); and finally the magazine. My mother is an editor, full of words, so she has always been a bit shocked that I didn't take after her. My dad is an architect, full of visuals. He says I inherited his genes.

They both wonder where I got the reddish-blond hair and blue eyes. They're both dark: Mom like the Old People who lived in the Welsh hills; Dad like his Semitic ancestors. He says my looks are Irish, a throwback to my grandmother Katie's side of the family.

That year was a time of decision for me because I

turned thirty. "If you wait much longer to marry, you won't ever have children and that will be a tragedy," my mother warned. I wanted to point out to her the difference between something tragic and something just sad, but I let it go by. I had just emerged from a long but rather listless relationship and wasn't eager to start a new one. It encourages me that unmarried women friends who are my age or older don't seem to feel marriage is all that essential. Ten years ago, when we got together to drink wine and giggle and get a little tipsy, all we talked about were the men in our lives. Or the men not in our lives. Five years ago, we spent half the time discussing love affairs and the other half career choices. Now we are focused on careers, but we're not obsessed with them. We talk about books and plays and travel and restaurants and job promotions and networking. If one of us has a new boyfriend or announces impending marriage, we all say, "How wonderful, darling!" and get on with our lives.

I believed that I *would* marry and have children. There *is* family precedent. My great-grandmother, Maggie, was thirty when she married my great-grandfather. Her journal about their courtship is like a romance novel.

In the last few years, working at the magazine and spending vacations in Europe, I got to know three first-rate photographers, all British, all living in London, who asked me to think about representing them. One is a terrific travel photographer, one is great at food (so ad agencies love him for product shots), and one does those dramatic grainy news photos—the kind that win Pulitzer Prizes. They all know each other—it's a small, chummy world—and they got together and asked me to come to live in London and be their agent. They even had a name picked out for me: SusanPix. I loved it.

Ralph and Flo—the travel photographer and his wife— met me at Heathrow. A cold rain was falling and I remembered the chilled-to-the-bone weather London gets in winter. "Not the best time of year here," Ralph offered ruefully. "You could have waited for spring."

"But I wanted to come in January. A new year, a new start."

As we drove into London, Ralph told me he was in the running for a really lucrative job—a photo shoot of Paris for one of the weekend newspaper supplements.

Flo whined a little. "They're leaning to a French photographer. Some guy who knows all those *arrondissements* tourists won't stay in and the cheap little restaurants tourists don't eat at. You have to do a real selling job with that editor, Susan, because Ralphie just doesn't know the *unknown Paris.* He's more the *known Paris* type."

Suddenly, I remembered my mother telling me about working on a book about Paris. "The art director wanted to use a photo of something *different* on the book cover—not the same old cliché of the Eiffel Tower. But I saw some research that said people who love Paris don't want something different; they want the Eiffel Tower."

"I think we can sell that editor," I said. "Get out your shots of the Eiffel Tower."

"The Eiffel Tower? That's an awful cliché."

"Just get them out, please."

They drove me to Kensington, where my photographers had all kicked in for the first month's rent of a furnished apartment. Tiny, they had warned me; not much more than a bed-sitter, but a great location, right near Kensington Gardens and Kensington Palace. "You can wave at the Princess of Wales, dear," Flo had written to me.

Without once circling the block, we found a parking place right across the street from the apartment. Try doing *that* in New York City, I thought. My flat was on the third floor but there was an elevator, the old kind where you have to yank the door open and pull across the grill. It was so small that we had to make two trips; first Ralph with the suitcases and the key, then Flo and I with the tote bag and umbrellas.

Ralph was inside. As soon as he heard the elevator, he threw the door open. "Welcome to SusanPix London!" Even here on the top floor, where the maids' rooms used to be, the ceilings were pretty high. Even on this rainy day, you could tell the place was going to be sunny. There was even a window box. "We stocked the pantry," Ralph announced. "And the fridge." He uncorked a bottle of champagne and filled two jelly glasses and a teacup. "Cheers!"

"I'm going to love it here," I said. "I'm going to love London." And somehow I knew I would.

The next two months turned out to be the coldest in memory. It snowed a lot, too, which the British aren't accustomed to. They can deal with icy temperatures and sleet, but three inches of snow on the ground is a

cataclysm. *The Times* was full of little news flashes like "Miss Martina Twidgett of Tewkinham-on-the-Wold was found frozen to death yesterday morning beneath the bird feeder in her garden. Miss Twidgett had apparently gone out in her dressing gown to replenish the feeder, and lost her way in the snow."

The Princess of Wales warmed the winter for us, though. (I think of her as Princess Di, but I never say that out loud.

Everyone adores her, but at the same time they are very respectful.) She has been visiting clinics that treat patients with AIDS. It's a fairly mysterious disease that has come from nowhere and attacks homosexuals. Some people call it "the Gay Plague"; there is no known cure. Yet Princess Di wades right in and shakes hands. Doesn't she worry about giving the virus or whatever it is to the princes?

I began going to church on Sundays at the Queen's Chapel, right across from St. James's Palace. My parents made sure I experienced both of their religions and studied the Bible, but didn't dictate a choice; by the time I was in my teens, I decided to be a Unitarian. Anglican services speak to me, and the music at the chapel is gorgeous—a choir of men, and boys with those sweet, soaring soprano voices. The chapel is one of my father's favorite places in London, designed by Inigo Jones in 1625 or something like that for Henrietta Maria, Catholic wife of Charles I. Of course, the chapel is now totally Anglican, and when the priest invites us to "prayer," the word is about four syllables long. One day, after the service, I heard two English women in the vestibule discussing the ordination of a woman as an Episcopal bishop in San Francisco. They were shocked.

My business was growing. Ralph did get the Paris job. I shared my research with the editor and persuaded him to feature either the Eiffel Tower or Notre Dame. I got Ralph a lot of other assignments, too, and Flo stopped whining. We landed the food photographer a job doing all the package photographs for a cereal company. And, best of all, I convinced *The Guardian* to send the news photographer to Alaska to cover the aftermath of the *Exxon Valdez* oil spill.

One Saturday morning in April, spring arrived in London. Kensington Gardens and Hyde Park were all green and shiny. A brigade of official gardeners was out pruning and digging and planting. People were sitting on newspapers or blankets on the damp grass, blinking in the sunshine. "One ray of sun and we Brits go barmy," my fishmonger said. I decided to give myself the day off, take a long walk, and visit some art galleries.

Time Out reported favorably on two exhibitions: one of Richard Avedon celebrity photos, another of nineteenth-century sculpture. I wanted to check on the first for professional reasons. The Victorian sculpture, at a gallery on Mount Street, intrigued me personally.

I walked through Hyde Park along Rotten Row, where the riders were out, most of them all proper in jodhpurs and bowlers; some of them looking American in jeans and flannel shirts. The air smelled wonderfully of lilacs and manure. There were even early boaters on the Serpentine. At

Hyde Park Corner, I went through the subway to get across to Piccadilly. I still have to remind myself that the Underground is a subway and a subway is an underpass.

The Avedon exhibit was jammed; celebrity photos always attract a crowd. Marilyn Monroe looking vulnerable, Elizabeth Taylor looking seductive, "Dovima with Elephants," "Nastassja Kinski and the Serpent." More than a hundred photographs, probably too many to take in properly.

Shepherd Market for lunch. I chose a little French café, ordered *moules marinières* and a glass of Chardonnay. I ordered in French and the waiter told me, also in French, that my pronunciation was quite passable. So my junior year in Lille was worth *something*.

I wasn't going to let the Spencer Gallery intimidate me, even though it was on Mount Street near the Connaught. This is Millionaire's Row, not only for hotels, but art and antiques. The gallery was of course on the ground floor of a grand old mansion. No signage except a discreet little metal plaque next to the door. I rang and someone inside buzzed me in. Most galleries have a series of rooms; here there was just one. Once upon a time, it must have been a great hall or a ballroom or something important. And I was the only person in it.

The space was a perfect backdrop for any work of art.

Elegantly simple white walls that went up forever. Casually scattered Mies chrome-and-leather chairs clearly not meant for sitting. And exactly seven pieces of Victorian sculpture, each on its own pedestal in its own space, each with its own light source, designed to highlight its best feature.

The first piece was quintessential nineteenth century: a mourning nymph weeping over an urn. The subject was a Victorian cliché, but the grief of this woman was real. Her body was young; her face was old, a *mater dolorosa*. I stood there, thinking how contemporary the figure was. I heard footsteps on the marble floor, and turned.

He looked British, with a kind of young Prince Charles air, sandy hair, craggy face, tweed jacket. He came toward me. "Hullo."

"Hi," I said, American to the core. And instantly regretted it.

"I'm Owen Spencer." We shook hands. Good handshake, I thought. Good hands.

"So this is your gallery." I was impressed.

"My family's gallery, actually."

"Owen is a Welsh name, isn't it? I know because my great-grandfather was an Owen. Are you Welsh?"

"No, straight English on both sides. You haven't told me your name as yet. Are you Welsh?"

"I'm sorry." I put out my hand to him again. "Susan Gottlieb. About one-eighth Welsh. My great-grandfather Owen would have said the best eighth."

"The name Owen has been a tradition in our family for about a century. The firstborn son is always named Owen."

"I like it," I said. "It's a strong name."

We stood there just looking at each other. Owen broke the silence. "I saw you hovering over *Mourning Goddess*. Did she speak to you?"

"Yes, she told me she will never be happy again, she will mourn every day until she dies. Owen, how come she is so real, so *now*?"

He looked pleased. "That's exactly the reason that I wanted her. The artist who sculpted her was also a painter, and he was working on a state portrait of Victoria when Albert died. He wrote in his journal that he saw the real agony of a woman who would never be young again, never in love again. Just as you said, Susan, she will never be happy again."

Owen took me on a tour of the other six sculptures, his hand on my arm. There was a sizzle of electricity between us that made it hard for me to concentrate on what he was telling me, the special story behind each one. I forced a thought into my head, offered it to him. "It's surprising to find them all carved in wood; I had expected something more Victorian-ly eternal, like marble."

He looked pleased again. "Marble is such an *Italian* medium. Just the way bronze is a French one. But wood . . . wood is at the heart of all things English." He completed the tour. "I have just one other comment," he announced. "Even though you and I have just met, I must tell you that you are the most beautiful woman in the world."

I was frozen in place, like one of the statues. He asked if he had offended me. "Oh, no, you just surprised me. No one ever said that to me before. And . . ."

"And?" he prompted.

"Family legend has it that my great-grandfather said exactly those words to a woman he had never met before, and told her it was ordained that they be married."

"And they were?"

"No."

"Well, Susan Gottlieb, I don't know what the future holds for us, but it is certainly ordained that we have dinner together tonight. If you have other plans, you'll have to break them." I didn't want to seem too available, wanted to protest that of course I had plans, but just shook my head. "I'll pick you up at eight. Don't dress. Not formal." He took me outside, asked me what my address was, put me in a cab, told the driver where to take me, and waved good-bye.

By six o'clock, every piece of clothing I owned was on my bed. What did he mean by "don't dress," and "not formal"? My favorite little black dress was too dressy, I thought, and anyway, how would I dare wear a cliché for a date with a man who collected wood sculptures. The navy suit was too casual, and how could I go casual for a man who spent his days in a marble palace? I decided on a shimmery rose silk dress almost the 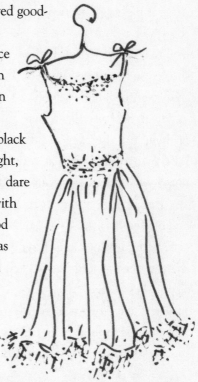 color of my hair, a dress I'd bought at Bloomy's just before coming to London. On sale, and it still cost a fortune, but I had spotted it from the top of the escalator and determined to buy it before I even saw the price.

I shampooed my hair and blew it dry, something I never do, and for good reason. It got all frizzy and unkempt, with the left side higher than the right. The more I brushed and blew, the worse it looked. "Don't you dare start crying, Susan," I lectured myself in the bathroom mirror, then got into the shower and rewashed my hair. I prayed it would be no more than slightly damp by the time Owen got there.

He arrived exactly on time, and with flowers. Tulips, nine of them, not the expected dozen. The family I lived with in Lille had taught me that a proper bouquet has an *uneven* number of flowers. I was impressed by Owen's sophistication.

"Your dress almost matches your hair," he said approvingly, and offered his arm. "May I take you to dinner?"

The taxi went along Knightsbridge and Piccadilly, skirting the same route I had walked earlier; but now Owen was sitting beside me. We passed the Ritz, turned into Bury Street, entered one of London's most beautiful small squares, and stopped in front of an eighteenth-century building.

"I love St. James's Square," I said, "but I never knew there was a restaurant here."

"It's a club, actually. The East India Club. I decided to take you here because it's Saturday, so they allow women in the bar. It's called the American Bar, by the way, so you'll feel right at home." He steered me through the lobby, hung with plaques honoring club members who had served their country in far-flung battles, and into a small bar that looked very

British to me. The bartender was polishing glasses. "Good evening, Andrew."

"Good evening, Mr. Spencer, good to see you, sir, as always. Will it be a dirty martini? And the lady?" Owen looked at me for approval. "Sure," I said, all-American again, and again regretted it. "Yes, lovely. I've never had a dirty martini before. Why is it called that?" And why, I wondered, am I babbling on?

"It's made with the juice of the olives in the jar. That gives the drink a sort of 'dirty' color. Thanks, Andrew." I was about to sit at one of the bar stools, but Owen carried the drinks to a banquette, went back to the bar for a glass bowl of potato chips, and sat down next to me. "Here's to your first dirty martini." We clicked glasses. "And have a crisp. The second-best crisps in the world."

"What are the first-best?"

"The crisps at the Hassler Bar. Ever been to Rome?"

"Yes, but not to the Hassler."

"Well, when we go there, that's where we'll stay. The Wirths, who own it, are old family friends."

"Oh," I said, flirting a little. "I didn't know we were going to Rome."

"I didn't know either," Owen said. "It's fun to imagine, though. We can go anywhere we like. What's the most romantic city in the world?" He didn't stop for my answer. "Venice, of course. But only if you know where to stay. We'll stay at a gorgeous old palazzo with just a few guest rooms. Room number nine has views over the Grand Canal that go on forever—the Rialto Bridge on the left, straight across the canal to the Rialto Market. All of Venice passes by right under your windows. We'll never have to leave the room." I knew my face was warm and took another sip of the martini, aware that I was drinking it too fast. "So we'll definitely go to Venice." He considered that for a moment, decided he was right, and nodded. "Yes, and when white truffles are in season."

"Ah," I said, and thought to myself that I had now progressed from babbling to muteness. I groped for something to say. "What's the *second-most* romantic city?"

"Paris," he answered instantly, pleased at the question. "I

know it sounds trite. Paris is a very romantic city. But only if you know—"

"Where to stay," we finished together. My voice had returned. Aha, I told myself. I know exactly why I felt such a strong attraction. Visual impact is important to me, without question, and Owen Spencer was unquestionably a good-looking man. But it was his sureness, his certainty that beguiled me. I had always been poor at ballroom dancing, yet I knew instinctively that, in Owen's arms, I would never miss a step.

He grinned at me. "You know they're working on that tunnel under the Channel. When it's finished, we'll just hop on a train and be in Paris for lunch. I always rent the same apartment on the Ile Saint-Louis. It's the most charming neighborhood in all of Paris—everything you want on one little street—butcher, baker, probably a candlestick maker if you look—and the world's best ice cream."

"And after we spend a few days in Paris, we will drive to Normandy." I wanted to show him I knew a little something of the world, too. "We will stay at the most romantic small hotel in all of France, in the hills overlooking Honfleur, a farmhouse where Monet used to paint. And we will have lunch in Villerville-sur-Mer. Do you know Villerville?"

He shook his head.

"There is a restaurant on the harbor where they make the best *soupe de poisson* in all the world."

Owen looked at me approvingly. "We're even," he said. "And you have just proved that we will travel very well. Like fine wine." He stood and escorted me into the dining room.

It was a large room, all crystal and candles and silver. Although almost every table was taken, the place was amazingly quiet. The guests conversed in muted undertones, the waiters trod softly, the busboys removed plates reverently, like servers at a mass. Even the trolley that held the roast beef rolled silently, and its silver cover was not permitted to clang.

"I suggest the lamb," Owen said. "It's from Wales. And Welsh lamb is . . ." He caught my eye and grinned again, not even apologetically. "Well, it's not the best lamb in the world, but it's damned good. As soon as you told me you were part Welsh, I knew I would bring you here for the lamb."

I grinned back. "Welsh lamb. Perfect."

"And a Bordeaux, I think." While Owen and the sommelier conferred, I looked around the room, hung with portraits of men in uniform, all of them be-ribboned and be-sashed, and some even be-wigged. It was a glorious meal, as Owen had promised. We ate the lamb and drank the wine and shared some cheese. And by the time dinner was over, I had begun to be a little in love with him.

He walked up the steps with me to my front door and kissed me. "May I come up?"

It took every bit of willpower I had, and some I didn't know was there, to resist. "No, Owen." Then I blurted, "Not yet."

"You're right," he agreed, and walked back down the steps. As I was putting the key in the lock, he called from the street. "Susan. Don't forget about Venice."

I tossed and turned and thought about him; at three o'clock the next morning, I dialed New York. I knew my mother would still be awake; she answered on the second ring. "Darling, it's the middle of the night in London. Is anything wrong?"

"Nothing is wrong at all, Mom. But you know everything about everything. So tell me . . ."

"Yes?"

"When is white truffle season in Venice?"

I moved in with Owen a month later, on May 21 to be exact. We had been seeing each other every day since we met, so living together seemed the natural next step. It *was* a quick decision, but that was apparently a family trait. Jessica Lavery had implored my great-grandfather Owen not to be so hasty.

I knew, for I had read all her letters to him. Owen had hidden them away and gave them to Grandfather James just before he died. He admitted that keeping the letters was the only secret he ever kept from his Maggie, but he couldn't bear to burn them.

The one debate Owen and I had was whether he should move into my flat or I should move into his. There wasn't much to discuss, really, since his apartment was larger and he had lots more stuff—furniture, clothing, books, artwork. Owen picked me up in a rented van and within a few hours we had unpacked and were cooking dinner in *our* place, on Markham Street, right off King's Road in Chelsea.

We watched the news before dinner, saw the protests beginning in Tiananmen Square, and learned the Chinese had declared martial law in Beijing. "It looks serious," I said. "It's going to get worse," Owen agreed. Two weeks later, the army brought in the tanks.

One of the unexpected fillips of our relationship was the enjoyment we found in each other's work. We were constantly going to gallery openings and receptions all over London, and Owen made sure I met all the appropriate editors. He liked all three of my photographers, helped me dream up assignments for them, and suggested the angle that might interest a magazine. He even introduced me to a fashion photographer, a fairly well-known woman. She had just broken up with her lover, who also happened to be her rep, so she joined SusanPix. Suddenly, I was making enough money to splurge and take Owen to Gordon Ramsay's for lunch on his birthday.

And I gave Owen at least one good idea for an exhibition. I was wandering around Chelsea one day and discovered that J. M. W. Turner had spent his last years, in the 1840s, at 119 Cheyne Walk. I knew almost nothing about Turner, read a biography out of curiosity, and found out the Chelsea years were unhappy ones for him. The Pre-Raphaelites had come into favor and he had fallen out. He kept painting, though, and turned to watercolors, a medium most artists then considered trivial. Some of his most important works date to that decade. "Lots of them are in private collections," I told Owen breathlessly. "Nobody has ever seen them. We could arrange to borrow them. It would get a lot of attention."

"It would take an immense amount of work," Owen groaned, but he looked interested.

"We'll do it together."

"Susan, we'll always do everything together." And that was how Owen proposed to me.

Owen took me to visit his parents. "They're just back from *months* in China and Japan looking for treasures for the gallery. I've told them all about you, and they're eager to meet the bride-to-be," he said. "They're prepared to like you." Kensington Court is what they refer to in London as "a mansion block," splendid old apartment buildings. The Spencers looked like they belonged there: elegant, easy, accessible. "We invited you to tea," Annabelle Spencer said, "but I am having a glass of Pinot Blanc. Susan?" I joined her; Owen and his father (also an Owen) had martinis, which Owen mixed. We talked about everything.

"I'm taking Susan to the Cotswolds for the weekend," Owen announced. "We four clearly have a good time together. Why don't you join us?"

"I wish we could, but we're going to Wales," his mother said.

"Of course, I should have known." Owen turned to me. "My parents own a little cottage near a town in the west of Wales. It's been in the family for over a hundred years."

"My grandparents bought it before the turn of the century," the elder Owen explained. "It was my grandmother's idea. For some reason, she fancied having a cottage in Wales, and found this one."

"Perhaps you two will take the cottage for Christmas," Annabelle suggested. "I would give it to you for your honeymoon, but Owen tells us you are both bent upon Venice."

"Oh, yes," I said. "Christmas in Wales would be lovely."

"And Owen told us you have Welsh roots," Annabelle continued. "So it would be a homecoming of sorts."

In August, we drove to Stratford for a matinee performance of *Othello*, with Ian McKellen as Iago and Willard White, the famous opera baritone, as the Moor. McKellen wrote in the program notes that the trick to playing Iago was to convince the audience—not just Othello, but the whole audience— that the character is sincere. And he did it.

The production was over three hours long, so we had decided to have dinner and spend the night in Stratford. Over dinner, we talked about the theater, plays we remembered, actors we loved. Of course we mourned Laurence Olivier, who had recently died. His favorite Olivier performance, Owen told me, was Henry V. "He could persuade me to go once more into the breach."

"My favorite Olivier is his Richard III. If I had been Lady Anne, I would have succumbed, too. Owen, I'm so glad that we both love the theater."

"It's probably in my genes," Owen answered. "My great-grandmother was an actress."

"Was she famous?"

"One of the great actresses of her day. A well-known playwright created a play just for her, and it was a huge success in London sometime in the 1870s. She married my great-grandfather, Reginald Spencer, and they had a son, the first of our family Owens."

We were married on October 20 in the Spencers' apartment, in front of the great mantel, which was banked with flowers for the occasion. Just our families were there; my father gave me away, my mother was my matron of honor, and Owen's father was his best man. It was a simple ceremony, sort of "low" Church of England, just what Owen and I wanted and agreeable to all the parents.

We flew to Venice the next morning and stayed at Owen's favorite small hotel, with views up, down, and across the Grand Canal, just as he had promised. White truffles were in season, as promised. And Venice was indeed the most romantic city in the world. But I was already thinking about Christmas in Wales.

One blustery Sunday in late November, we decided to spend the afternoon at the National Gallery, and wandered for hours from Italian *quattrocento* to Renaissance Spain. Happily worn out, we had a cup of tea in the museum café. "Which one shall I buy for you?" I asked. It was a game we always played after going to any museum or gallery. "The Duccio *Annunciation*, I think," Owen answered. "How about you?"

"I am a woman of simple tastes. The El Greco *St. Jerome*."

"That may not even be an El Greco. It's only 'attributed to.'" Owen always worried about authenticity.

"I don't care. I want him over our fireplace."

"Done." We stopped in at the museum shop, and I spotted a gorgeous porcelain Christmas ornament: one of the Three Kings, elongated, Byzantine, almost an El Greco figure. "Oh, let's buy him for our Christmas tree."

As the clerk wrapped the figure, Owen said: "It's probably too delicate for our tree, Susan. My family has a tradition that a Christmas tree should always be outside."

"Where it can look up to God," I added. "So does my family." We looked at each other for a long moment. "I always thought it was a Thomas family tradition."

"And I always thought it was a *Spencer* tradition," Owen said. "I've never heard of it before outside my family. And now yours. Mysterious."

"Well, it's one more thing we have to share," I said. But I wondered about the coincidence.

In early December, I told Owen that I had a surprise for him, a decoration for our Christmas tree in Wales. I had planned to wait until Christmas Eve, but found I was as eager as a four-year-old.

Owen caught the note of excitement in my voice. "I love surprises. May I have it now?"

"Oh, yes," I said, and gently handed him the angel, wrapped in the old blue woolen shawl. "She has been in our family for a century now. My mother sent her to me, just as *her* mother did to her, to be at the top of our tree for our first married Christmas together."

Owen unwrapped the shawl and I heard his sharp intake of breath. "What is it?"

"The angel's eyes," he answered. "They say my great-grandmother had lavender eyes."

The Spencers invited us for pre-Christmas dinner before we left for Wales. "Owen has been telling me about his famous great-grandmother," I told them. "Why did she have such a passion for Wales?"

"Nobody really knows," Owen's father said. "Reginald Spencer could have afforded to buy her a great old manor house in Surrey, or anyplace else, for that matter. So the family never did understand why she chose to bury herself in a little Welsh mining town called Llanelli."

Llanelli. It reverberated inside my head and suddenly all the pieces came together. I could barely whisper the words. "What was your great-grandmother's name?" I asked Owen. But I knew the answer before he spoke.

"Jessica Lavery," he said.

We arrived at the house in Llanelli two days before Christmas. It was almost dusk, but the brook glinted white in the setting sun. "Glan Wynne suits this place, doesn't it?" Owen said softly. "White Glen." He pointed out the fir tree near the front door. "The tree from your great-grandfather's day was still standing when I was a boy," he remembered. "A giant, but it blew over in a winter storm and my parents planted this one in exactly the same place."

Owen took me through the little house, the house we now knew that Owen had built. In the bedroom was the headboard he had carved; the tiny cradle wrought with such hope and love. "And look at this, Susan," Owen urged. "My great-grandmother's writing desk. Rosewood. It should be in a museum."

The day before Christmas was cold but sunny; the light gleamed on the whitewashed walls of the cottage. We decorated the tree, and placed the angel at the top, in her place of honor. "She belongs here in Glan Wynne," Owen said.

"Yes," I agreed. "The angel has come home."

All day long, I was drawn to Jessica's writing desk. It felt comfortable to sit there, composing a letter to my mother in New York, telling her about these amazing events. Yet somehow, for me, the story still lacked an ending.

I glanced out the window, to the tree we had decorated this morning, to the angel at its top. She held my eye. "What is it?" I asked her. My mother told me a long time ago that the angel didn't speak very often, but when she did, it was important to listen. "She gave me the best advice of my life," my mother said.

The angel seemed to tell me what to do. On an impulse I reached inside Jessica's desk, pulled out a drawer, and felt around inside for the catch I knew must be there. I heard a click, and the secret compartment slid open, revealing my great-grandfather Owen's letters. They had been hidden there for over one hundred years, waiting for me to find them. Now I knew I could write the story. Now I knew I *must* write it.

At dusk, my Owen turned on the lights of the tree and without saying a word we went out and stood beside it. I looked up at the angel and thought of all the Christmases she had seen, watching over our family. Christmas is truly a season of magic and miracles, of birth and rebirth. It is a time to rejoice because we know that although night comes, we will never again be in darkness.

Owen took my hand. "*Cariad*," he said.

The baby girl who was born to us in the autumn had lavender eyes.

ACKNOWLEDGMENTS

*

Traditionally, women are the midwives and it is chiefly women I want to thank for working with me to give birth to this book. I am especially grateful to my sister, Susan Weston, and my mermaid sister in London, Susan Hunter Griggs, for suggestions about both plot and characters, and for criticism that was alway helpful and sometimes severe. Susan Griggs was there for me every day for months, read and commented on draft after draft, and painstakingly proofread the final manuscript. If this *Angel* has wings, she has fashioned them.

Anne Brewer and Margaret Brown were once again my cheerleaders, literary advisers, and muses from start to finish. Anne is an associate editor at Thomas Dunne Books, a division of St. Martin's Press. Margaret recently left St. Martin's to join her husband in Canada. We miss her.

It was a delight to work with my gentle new friend, artist

and gardener Abbie Zabar. Abbie has a green thumb with everything, including people. Her charming illustrations added a whole new dimension to this book.

Crescent Dragonwagon, who teaches us all about fearless writing, opened my eyes to the feisty character of Maggie. Carolyn Waters, assistant head librarian of the New York Society Library, led me to rich source materials about the Welsh in Pennsylvania.

I am grateful, as always, to Lynn Nesbit, who reined me in for an entire year to rewrite and revise. And, as always, thanks to my family at St. Martin's Press: Tom Dunne, Sally Richardson, Matthew Baldacci, Stephanie Hargadon, Laura Clark, Kerri Resnick for the delightful cover design, Mike Storrings for his contributions to the cover, Meg Drislane for unfailing good taste, Kathryn Parise for her elegant design, Christina MacDonald for uncanny copy editing, and the entire St. Martin's sales team for unflagging enthusiam.

Old friends and new at Hallmark Channel paid me the compliment of believing that *The Christmas Angel* would be just right for one of their treasured holiday movies. My thanks to Bill Abbott, Susanne McAvoy, Michelle Vicary, and especially to Randy Pope.

I am sure my loved ones wanted to say, "Oh no, not another book!" but they restrained themselves. Kate and Jenna Maas, Jen and Allen Jones, Harry R. Garvin, bless you.

*